RIVER MEETS THE SUN

A TALE OF ANINI & NOGAS

SHIRLEY SIATON PARABIA

PETER PARABIA

RIVER MEETS THE SUN
A Tale of Anini and Nogas

ISBN 978-621-96917-3-4 (hardcover)
ISBN 978-1-961052-43-7 (paperback)
ISBN 978-621-96917-4-1 (paperback, *limited release***)**

1st Edition, October 2025

Published by Inky Sword Book Publishing
Cover by Artscandare Book Design
Interior formatting by Champagne Book Design

Inky Sword Book Publishing
Barangay Quezon, Arevalo, Iloilo City 5000
Republic of the Philippines
inkysword.com

CONTENT WARNINGS

This story contains themes of grief, loss, and violence, including scenes of combat. It may be emotionally intense for some readers.

This book is recommended for readers 13 years old and above.

To Mayor Maxfil Pollicar
for believing in us

To Ms. Lourdes Pollicar
for welcoming us home

To our parents
Boy & Mimi
and
Rodrigo & Flora

To our children
Arya & Selene

To the people of Barangay Igtumarom

and

To the people of Anini-y,
Antique, Philippines

CONTENTS

RIVER MEETS THE SUN

PROLOGUE

THE MOUNTAIN HOLDS ITS BREATH WITH THE DAWN. Long before the first flame of the sun touches the peaks, I am awake, kneeling beside the still pool beneath the cliffs. Mist hangs in the air like memory, and the wind carries the scent of ayangile, smoke, and something older. Something unsettled.

The sky has not turned, but I feel the change upon us.

Today, the lowlanders climb.

Datu Oyong of Tinigbasan rides with his gold-slicked guards and sharpened smiles, bringing peace wrapped in expectation. He comes not to speak, but to measure. Not to honor, but to remind.

A treaty of friendship with Kalisidlan, they called it. A promise of protection from one of Hamtic's oldest kingdoms to our much smaller tribe tucked away in the terraces of the far north.

Oyong honors it every sun-cycle with a visit. With gifts and celebration.

Kalisidlan is a mountain flame. Tinigbasan hopes to trap it in a lamp.

But we are not tame.

I press my palms to the cold earth. The stone hums beneath my skin, faint and patient, the beating heart of the mountain itself. It does not speak in words, but I have learned to listen.

Behind me, the tribe stirs. Fires are lit. Armor checked. Spears oiled. The younger warriors walk tall today. They think peace is a stage, not a blade. But I have seen the way power cloaks itself in hospitality. I have seen what happens when kings arrive with drums and leave with names carved into the land.

The chieftain called me last night. He told me to be present when the caravan arrives. I am of age now, the protector of the northern ridge—the most treacherous paths of the peaks.

"Let them see you," he said. "Let them wonder."

I asked nothing in return.

Not because I serve without question, but because I have seen what the wind does to those who wait too long to rise.

I stand now, quiet, alone. The water reflects only shadow.

They do not know what I am.

Not yet.

But something in me awakens with the dawn. If feels like something old, like steel drawn from stone. I feel it coiling beneath my ribs.

Not rage. Not fear. Just readiness.

There is a legend the elders whisper around firelight.

A tale of the river and the sun.

How when they meet, the world must break before it can be made new.

I used to think it was a tale for children.

Now, I wonder if it was a warning.

A bird cries far off. The air sings with the rustle of the trees and crops. A thin breath of warmth creeps through the mist.

Somewhere beyond the valley, the river stirs.

The air tastes faintly of promise.

I know, without question, that something ends with the sunrise.

CHAPTER 1

Jewel of the Isles

ANINI

THE RIVER FOG LINGERS LONGER THAN IT SHOULD. I rise before the sun, as always. I move in the shadows of my hut as I have for many sun-cycles, my breath and footsteps as one. By the time a ripple of fiery red filters through the clouds in the east, I am already bathed and dressed.

Before I begin my day, I read the scroll once more.

My dearest Anini,
The river has grown restless. It asks when you will return. Each dawn, I light the lamp facing the eastern skies and think of the child who once chased fireflies along these banks.
The wind carries your name again,

*but more willfully this cycle of the sun.
I do not know what it means, only that
the water always remembers you.*

*I look forward to your visit as I do
every season, daughter of the currents.
The river waits, and, as always, so do I.*

— Agdan

I roll the parchment back carefully, then press it to my heart for a moment. It feels warm and alive, one of the only real things I can hold and never doubt.

Agdan used to be my tutor. A seemingly ageless shaman and scholar, he was brought to court from the river temple by my mother to teach me to read and write. But that was a long time ago; he'd long since returned. I visit him often, once a season at least, to bring scrolls and trinkets of knowledge from Tinigbasan's allies and visitors.

I put the scroll away in a chest next to my sleeping mats, thinking of my trip to the temple in the coming days. My father or the captain of the Royal Guard would always accompany me, but this time I insisted on traveling on my own, with my own court. It was a victory hard fought against the Datu and his council of advisors and elders.

By the time I leave my palace and stand on the terraces, the valley glimmers in silver and smoke, as if the world itself hesitates to wake. From here, I can see the bridges. They appear like stone veins across the water, pulsing with torches from the night before. Tinigbasan stirs slowly, like a great beast stretching in its sleep.

The courtiers will call it beautiful when the sun rises. They always do.

But I know better. Beauty, here, is something demanded. Something to be polished daily. Something that is rehearsed and repeated until even the land learns to smile for its rulers.

I am called the Jewel of Hamtic, a gem born of the glittering isles and its currents, though sometimes I think that only means I am meant to be locked away.

Attendants move through the courtyard like restless shadows. Drums wait to sound departure. My father, Datu Oyong, is preparing to ride for the mountain village of Kalisidlan before the next tide turns.

I have asked to go with him. Twice.

Both times, he laughed.

"It is a hard road," he said last night. "The climb is steep and fraught with raiders. We heard tell of more movement from the Dumalog, going inland this time. Dust and danger are no place for a jewel."

"Then take me as steel," I told him.

He only smiled. The kind of smile that ends conversations.

Now I stand by the rail, watching as his guards tighten the last leather straps on the saddles of their water beasts. The air smells of oil and yesterday's rain. My nurse, Lira, stands beside me, her hands tucked neatly into her sleeves. She has served me since I was a child. Her husband, Captain Mion, leads Father's Royal Guard.

Lira watches them with the faint disapproval of a woman used to letting men believe they command more than they do.

"If your father had sense," she mutters, "he'd take you with him. At least you'd keep him from making speeches that sound like war songs."

"He says the journey will tire me."

She snorts. "The journey would tire *him*."

I hide my smile behind my sleeve. To the court, Lira is all politeness and decorum, but with me, she refuses to hold back.

I still like to believe it is something she promised my mother, Dayang Rumina, before the fevers took her from us when I was six.

"Besides," Lira continues, eyes narrowing at the cluster of visiting banners flapping by the southern gate, "you'll have your own battle to fight today. The king and prince from the merchant isles arrive by noon. Another suitor for the Datu's peace."

I glance toward the embroidered standards brought in by their envoy, red ships emblazed on gold seas. They shimmer like coins in sunlight.

Peace, lately, has begun to sound like a market bargain.

"They bring trade," Father said last night. "And trade brings safety."

But what he meant was alliances.

And what alliances mean, in every kingdom in Hamtic and beyond, is marriage.

"Just as well," Lira says dryly, "it's high time you had your own court of ladies and guards, Princess. Form your own council of scholars and advisors. Travel as a princess should. Visit the other islands, even beyond the straits. Let them see Tinigbasan has a jewel who shines on her own."

I know she is mostly teasing, but there's weight in her words.

Freedom disguised as courtesy.

Father overhears as he approaches, helm under his arm, armor gleaming like burnished dusk.

"Lira," he says with the patient fondness of a man too practiced at ignoring advice, "our princess has all the world she needs here. Besides, have I not already approved for her to travel to the river temple on her own upon my return?"

Lira bows low, though I catch the flicker of her smirk. "Of course, Datu. As you say."

He turns to me, his voice softening. "Watch over our guests. Speak wisely. And remember, even in silence, you represent our people."

"As always, Father," I reply.

He nods, then presses a kiss to my forehead. "Good girl."

He mounts the carriage tethered to two water beasts, and the drums thunder once, then again. The caravan begins to move, banners of deep brown and gold streaming toward the mist. Lira's husband rides on another beast at the head, his spear gleaming in the early morning light. The air fills with hoofbeats and chants of prayer from the palace shaman.

When they vanish beyond the gates, the silence that follows feels odd.

Too sudden. Too deep.

I look back toward the river. The fog hasn't lifted. It swirls low over the water like a curtain drawn across a secret.

Lira sighs. "And so begins another morning in Tinigbasan."

I straighten, already feeling the weight of the day ahead.

The foreign king, the calculating prince, the endless dance of politeness.

The Jewel of Hamtic, they call me.

I know a jewel cannot shine without light.

But I am starting to wonder what waits beyond the mountain.

And whose hand will bring the dawn.

CHAPTER 2

Nogas

THE MOUNTAIN PATH FOLDS INWARD LIKE A THROAT. Tall and dense ayangile lean close on both sides, their branches heavy with mist. The stones underfoot are damp, the air too quiet. From my perch halfway up the cliff, I can see the procession below. The gilded caravan of beasts and men winds through the narrow road like a slow vein of light against gray rock.

They move as lowlanders do. Loudly and confidently, believing that the treaty ceremony and celebrations protect them from danger.

They do not.

Their armor gleams against the green, too bright and careless for a place such as this. They are an announcement to the wilderness. An invitation.

Here we are. We have never bled for this soil.

I stand unseen on the ridge, blending into the earth and growth in my woven grass mask and clothing of dense brown weave. I know they will pass me on their way up the path but will never see the man in the brush.

I adjust my grip on the spear. The haft is cool, smooth, worn to my hand.

Then I smell it.

Smoke, but not ours. A faint bite of wood. Burned leather.

Raiders.

And the forest breathes out, shakily.

I see them then, only because I know where to look. They are shapes that should not move where light does not ripple. They are painted in ash and mud, skin smeared green and brown to vanish into moss and bark. Strips of fern and cloth hang from their belts to blur their outlines when they run.

They appear like ghosts of the forest.

They come for plunder. Or blood.

Or both.

The first arrow looses before the wind changes. I hear the whisper before the scream.

The shaft buries itself in the throat of a Tinigbasan rider at the rear. The lowlander gurgles, then falls.

Their beasts panic.

A second volley follows, silent until it sings through armor. The path becomes chaos. Men shout orders, shields rise too slow, the Datu's standard tilts.

The raiders erupt from both slopes at once. Deep green figures with painted faces, blades carved from boar bone and bronze. They howl like wolves, the sound raw enough to shake birds from the trees.

They are Dumalog. The salt-born. They are from the dead isles in the deepest shadows of the Hamtic sea. Their noises say it all. Water with force always crashes.

If they had been of the mountains, they would not make a sound at all.

And I am already moving.

I leap from the ledge, spear balanced in my hands. The drop is steep, but the mountain knows me. The rock catches my feet, slides, then lets me go. I fall the last few paces and land behind the first wave of raiders.

The impact stings through my knees, but I do not stop.

The closest one turns, eyes widening behind streaks of moss and soot.

He lunges. I twist. The spear flashes. His chest opens.

The others freeze for half a breath, confused by my mask, by my silence.

Then the sun breaks through the clouds.

I angle the blade just so, and light catches it, splintering across the bronze tip.

It blinds them for a heartbeat.

That is all I need.

I strike low, sweeping legs from beneath bodies, then drive the butt of the spear into a throat. Someone grabs my arm. I pivot, using his pull to turn, and the spear finds his ribs.

They come fast after that. Desperate, snarling, smelling of salt and animal hide.

I do not hear them as men. Only as rhythm.

Step. Spin. Strike.

Metal. Flesh. Air.

Blood spatters the stone in sharp arcs. The light gleams on every droplet before it falls.

One of them tackles me sideways. We roll over mud and stone, his dagger grazing my arm. I trap his wrist, force the blade back. His eyes meet mine through the mask slit, wild and frightened. I break his wrist, then his neck.

I rise again.

The Datu's men are faltering, overwhelmed. Mion, their captain, stands before his lord, a shield raised high, blood leaking from his shoulder. Three raiders corner him.

I run.

The world narrows to the sound of breath and steel. I hurl my spear.

It whistles through the air and catches one raider clean through the back. I tear it free as I pass him. The next lunges. I duck, ram the shaft through his stomach, and twist, feeling it catch bone.

The third hesitates. Too long. The sun hits the edge of my weapon again, a flash of white fire, and I drive the spear upward through his jaw.

Silence follows, ringing heavily.

My chest burns. Blood trickles from my arm, warm against the cold air. I pull the mask aside just long enough to breathe. The metallic scent of death thickens around me.

I look up. The last of the raiders are fleeing into the trees. Their paint makes them ghosts again. My body aches to follow, to finish it, but I do not.

This was not my war.

The wind hums softly through the carnage. The afternoon mist thins.

Around me, the path is red. Bodies of raiders and lowlanders alike lie tangled in the mud.

I wipe the spear clean against a fallen cloak, the gold sunlight still dancing along its length. The familiar warmth steadies me.

Captain Mion groans where he kneels, clutching his wound. The Datu of Tinigbasan crouches beside him, half armored, breathing hard, face pale with shock and pride. His guards stand uncertain, blades still drawn but hands trembling.

All of them stare at me.

Not one dares speak.

I stand amid the bodies, sunlight burning across my shoulders, blood still wet on my hands.

The Datu raises his eyes.

Our gazes lock.

For a long moment, neither of us moves.

Then the wind changes again, soft, almost cold, like the mountain exhaling after holding its breath too long.

And I know what he sees.

Not a man.

But a weapon the gods forgot to name.

CHAPTER 3

Cry of the River

Anini

The palace smells of wax and sweet oil. Perfume from foreign merchants hangs heavy over smooth stone floors and carved beams. In the middle of the Datu's hall, I sit amid perfectly polished low tables and intricately woven mats.

I keep my smile fixed as the visiting king bows low. He moves in a proud, practiced manner. His son follows, eyes measuring. Their clothes shimmer like fish scales, layers of gold silk embroidered with red ship sigils that gleam whenever light touches them.

Lira stands at my shoulder, silent, reading every gesture. I pour the tea and serve the cakes myself, as courtesy demands. The prince's fingers brush the cup too long when I hand it to him.

"Your people are blessed," he says. "To have a princess so radiant the sea itself envies her."

His father chuckles, all charm and teeth, as he gestures to the pile of gifts wrapped in silk at the center of the hall. "We bring the bounty of our isles as proof of friendship, Princess Anini. And perhaps a token of greater union."

I smile politely. "Tinigbasan welcomes friendship always. We have more need for peace than gold."

"Ah, but both are sweet when shared," the king replies. He raises his cup, his eyes never leaving mine.

Outside, the cicadas seem to hum louder. My skin prickles.

Then...

The light.

It cuts through the lattice window, sudden and merciless.

My eyes sting, my vision flooding white. I hear Lira's gasp as the cups tremble against the tray. A ringing fills my head, distant and high, like bells underwater. My pulse pounds against my temples. My throat tastes of metal.

"Princess?" Lira's voice pierces through the blur. "Princess, what's wrong?"

I blink, once, then again. I try to stand, but the world lurches. My knees buckle at the effort.

"I'm fine," I mutter, even as heat coils behind my ribs. "Just the sun."

But it is not the sun. Not as I have ever known it.

Something moves inside me. It feels bright, alive, *impossible.*

The air vibrates.

And the light does not fade.

It pulses.

It feels like something has seen me and chosen me in return.

Lira catches my arm. "You're pale as wax. Sit, before you fall."

I shake my head, then push myself to my feet.

"Please, Your Majesties," I say, forcing calm. "Forgive me. The air is heavy today. I shall find my bearings and return shortly."

The prince makes a move to get up. "Allow me to escort—"

"No. Thank you." My tone is gentle but final. "Rest, Your Majesty. Enjoy the tea. My lady will tend to me. An official of the court will be with you shortly. Forgive me."

Before they can insist, I bow and turn. Lira sweeps behind me, murmuring apologies to cover my retreat. Before we leave the room, I hear her ask one of the guards to fetch the trade advisor and his wife to entertain the merchant king.

Once outside, I breathe. I take in the smells of the sea and the faint tang of river moss. The light follows us, thinner now but still strange, still watching. My pulse thunders in my ears.

"Where are we going?" Lira asks softly.

I answer without hesitation. "The river."

We cross the courtyard, my eyes pulsing with each heartbeat. The stones shimmer like scales. By the time we reach the terraces, my head spins, but the sight roots me still.

The river stretches below, its surface gold-bright under a sky too pale for the afternoon. My steps pick up as we approach the bank.

I kneel and touch the water.

It feels warm and alive, thrumming under my fingers. It breathes against my palm. I taste metal in the air, hear the faint hiss of something bubbling beneath the current. The horizon glows.

For a breath, I swear I see the flash of a spear cutting through mist.

Like sunlight made blade.

I gasp, as if struck. Tears spill out of my eyes, hot and stinging.

Lira grips my shoulder. I turn to see her face losing color.

"Princess, what do you see?" she asks shakily.

"An omen," I answer raggedly. "It feels like…change, Lira."

"Change?" she echoes, bringing a small piece of cloth to wipe at my cheeks.

My chest feels tight, almost heavy, as I open my mouth to speak. "Send a messenger to my father. Tell him the sun broke through too early today. Tell him to…come home. Before it's too late."

Lira hesitates. "You think—"

"I don't think," I breathe. "I feel. Go."

She bows and runs.

I remain, staring eastward. The light dances over my skin, fevered and soft all at once.

In the distance, beyond the valley, the mountain seems to ripple, as if breathing in the heavy breeze.

And I, the river's daughter, feel the world tilt, slowly and irrevocably, toward something that will forever change its course.

CHAPTER 4

Fire of the Mountain

Nogas

T HE WIND STILL CARRIES THE SCENT OF BLOOD AND ash long after the battle ends.

I kneel beside a wounded guard, binding his arm with a strip torn from my cloak. His breath rattles, but he will live.

Around us, the survivors of the Datu's caravan move like men half-dreaming, gathering weapons, counting their dead. The warriors of Kalisidlan have reached us by now, helping the lowlanders gather their provisions into what remains of their carriages.

The Datu himself sits against a boulder, a torn golden cloak across his shoulders, his gaze steady despite the pain lining his face.

"Who are you, warrior?" he asks at last.

His voice is low and controlled. He sounds like a man too proud to reveal how close he came to dying.

I bow my head. "Nogas of the Kalisidlan, Datu. Protector of the northern ridge."

His eyes narrow, searching my face as though he might find deceit hidden in the scars. "You fight like no man I have seen."

"I fight as the mountain teaches," I say quietly. "With what it gives."

He studies me for a long breath, then nods. "Then today, the mountain saved Tinigbasan."

I do not answer. Praise is like sunlight. It fades quickly.

I work in silence. I help the wounded to their feet, guide their beasts from the wrecked path, and retrieve what supplies the raiders did not burn. When Captain Mion stumbles, I offer him my arm. He accepts with a grunt, pride too heavy to thank me aloud.

By the time the sun slips behind the ridges, the dead lowlanders are laid out with their faces to the sky. The slain Dumalog are taken into the forest by my kinsmen to be buried.

The Datu insists on walking the last stretch to the village, refusing a litter. I walk beside him, silent sentinel to a shaken king.

The path curves downward into the valley. The watchfires of my people flicker ahead like amber eyes in the mist. When we cross the threshold of stone to the outer huts, the mountain chief, Bantawan, and his council wait in a circle.

I step back, letting the Datu speak first.

He does not waste words. "You have loyal men,

Chieftain, and a warrior touched by the gods. Tinigbasan is in your debt."

The chieftain bows slightly. "Our loyalty and friendship have always been yours."

Oyong's gaze shifts to me. "Then lend him to me. A warrior like this should not be hidden in the mountains."

The fire pops between them, a sound sharp as a blade drawn.

Bantawan's smile is slow and careful. "You ask for much, Datu."

"I offer peace," Oyong replies. "He will serve as my guard. My sword. A tethered blade to remind my court of the mountain's loyalty. And, of course, its strength."

A murmur ripples through the circle. I keep my face still, my heart silent.

The chieftain's eyes gleam in the firelight.

"Then he will go," Bantawan says at last, "but on one condition."

"Name it."

"He will not guard you. He will guard your heart."

Oyong frowns. "My heart?"

"Your daughter, Datu," the chieftain clarifies. "The Jewel of Hamtic."

Oyong hesitates only a moment. "If that is your price, so be it."

The agreement is sealed with the exchange of blades. Bronze for bronze, oath for oath. They tell me another rite will take place in Tinigbasan, as is custom for royals and their shields.

When the Tinigbasan men retire to the huts prepared

by the tribe for them, the chief gestures for me to follow him beyond the fires.

The oncoming night is sharp with damp leaves, smoke, and the lingering smell of blood. We stop at the ridge where the stars begin to spill like salt across the sky.

"The Princess of Tinigbasan has come of age," Bantawan says. "She needs a shield. You will be that."

"I would have preferred the front line," I admit. "Not a palace of whispers."

He chuckles softly. "The front line is easy. You see your enemy. You strike. But a court…the enemy wears perfume and smiles."

I say nothing. My hands still ache from the weight of the spear.

He glances sideways. "They call her Anini. Beautiful and clever. Courted by half the lords of the lowlands and the seas. I have it on good authority that she is hosting the king and prince of the merchant isles as we speak. The Datu keeps her locked behind manners and gold. You will for yourself see soon enough."

"I have not trained for that," I say simply. "Courtly games. Words dressed like knives. That is not my craft, Chieftain."

"Exactly," he answers. "That is why you must go. They have too many who play the game. They need one who cuts through their affectations."

I bow slightly. "If that is your command."

He places a heavy hand on my shoulder. "It is time for the isles to know of Kalisidlan, for our fire to reach those kept too long in the shadows and the cold."

I meet his gaze.

"When the river meets the sun, the world changes," I say softly.

Bantawan smiles, then nods once. "Perhaps this is where it begins, Nogas."

His gaze turns to the horizon, where dusk begins to edge the mountains in pale flames.

Although I do not yet know her beyond rumor, I feel the echo of that light in my chest.

And it burns.

CHAPTER 5

Chains of Freedom

Anini

Thε voices of the children rise and fall as they sound out the words, each tumbling like pebbles in a stream.

We have set up our small reading circle under the balete tree by the village square, the cool afternoon breeze carrying the smells of damp leaves and dried ink. More than twenty of them, from ages six to ten, sit cross-legged around me, bamboo tablets balanced on their knees.

"Slowly," I remind them, smiling. "Let the words walk, not run."

A few giggles ripple through the group. Lira sits nearby, mending a torn hem while pretending not to listen.

When the last line of the poem is read aloud, I close the scroll.

"That was *The Song of the River,*" I tell them. "Written

by my mother, Dayang Rumina, in honor of the temple and banks where she grew up. It reminds us that water remembers every stone it touches. Every path, every name."

The children bow low before scampering off, chattering and barefoot, the way light scatters across water.

It's peaceful for a moment. Almost too peaceful.

Then I hear the sound of hooves.

A messenger mounted on a water beast approaches the clearing, breathless, dust clinging to his hair and armor. He is from my father's court, based on his garb of dark brown and silver.

"Princess!" he calls out, dismounting before the beast even stops. He drops to one knee, his chest heaving. "Your father is returning from the mountains. I was sent by Lady Lira with your message for the Datu, but he and the caravan are already on their way back."

Relief flares through me. "He's safe?"

"Yes, Princess," he says quickly, then hesitates. "But…"

"But what?"

He glances at Lira before meeting my eyes again. "There was an ambush on the mountain road. Raiders. Many dead. The Datu lives only because a warrior from the vassal tribe intervened."

My heart stumbles once, then steadies. "A warrior?"

He nods. "A young man. The Datu has…brought him back. He says the warrior is to remain in Tinigbasan. By his command."

Lira arches a brow. "Another suitor, perhaps?"

The messenger shakes his head. "No, Lady. A shield, I believe." He swallows, then adds, "For the Princess Anini."

For a moment, the word doesn't sink.

A *shield*?

For me?

Vaguely, I hear the messenger telling Lira in a soft voice that the captain of the Royal Guard rode back with the Datu. She sighs in relief, then holds out a hand.

I take it and rise slowly, gathering my things. "My father must be exhausted. I'll see him."

Lira mutters, "And by *see*, you mean *scold.*"

But she follows me anyway.

The Datu's palace is busy with movement when I enter.

Guards unloading packs, healers tending to wounded men, servants carrying bowls of water and steaming broth. The air is thick with the scent of earth and sweat.

I push through it, ignoring the bows and murmurs, until I find my father in the inner hall. He sits tall despite the bandage around his arm, his face drawn but triumphant.

"Anini," he says, standing as I approach. "You need not have come so quickly. I'm fine."

"I heard," I answer softly as he puts his arm around me. "And I'm grateful."

My gaze flicks over the men in the hall.

Then it stops.

Right away, I know it's him.

The warrior of Kalisidlan.

He stands near the steps, silent and unmoving as stone. Tall and lean like lightning, hair falling to his broad shoulders, his dark tunic of heavier weave than the garb of lowlanders. A spear rests across his back, its bronze tip glinting faintly like captured sunlight.

Something in me falters.

"This is the warrior who saved us," Father says.

He bows slightly. "Datu."

Then his eyes meet mine. They look like river rocks of deepest gray, carved into his face that's all stillness, shadow, and blade.

"Princess Anini." He drops to one knee before me, lowering his head. "An honor to be in your presence. They call me Nogas."

I incline my head, perfectly measured, though my pulse betrays me. "Welcome to Tinigbasan, Nogas. Thank you for saving my father and his men."

My father smiles faintly. "He will serve as your shield from now on. Wherever you go, he goes."

The words hit harder than I expect, coming from my father's lips.

"My shield?"

"Yes." He doesn't notice the edge in my voice. "A reward for his valor. And, of course, a gesture of goodwill from the mountain tribe. You will need protection as tensions rise. With what happened in Kalisidlan, your safety is now of paramount importance to all of Hamtic."

"Of course," I say sweetly, though my throat burns. "How thoughtful."

I bow, turn, and walk away before the heat behind my eyes can betray me.

Lira finds me in the garden, pacing beneath the tamarind trees.

"You walked out on your father," she says, folding her arms. "I've seen storms less dramatic."

"I walked out before I said something I would later regret," I mutter. "He's appointed me a *shield*, Lira. As if I were a child."

"You're not a child, Anini," she says mildly. "You're a princess. And a shield means freedom, not chains."

I stop pacing. "Freedom?"

She sighs. "If you have a personal guard, you can finally go where you please. Into the markets. Even the coast and the outer villages. You may even visit the nearby isles on your own. You'll have someone to blame if the council complains."

"That's your argument? Turn my leash into a banner?"

"It's better than snarling at your father in front of half the court."

I glare at her, but she meets it evenly.

"He nearly died on that mountain, Princess," Lira says. "Let your father feel like he's doing something to keep you safe. It costs you nothing but pride. Take your new shield to the river temple, for a start. Have Agdan complete the rites of servitude on your visit."

Before I can answer, a deep voice breaks through the quiet.

"Princess. I beg your pardon."

Lira's head snaps around. "Mion!"

He stands at the edge of the path, arm bandaged, face pale but smiling faintly.

Lira rushes to him, scolding even as she fusses. "You're supposed to be resting! Look at you! Bleeding and limping!"

"I've missed your temper," Mion murmurs, kissing her forehead before bowing to me. "Princess. Forgive my intrusion."

"You're always welcome," I tell him gently. "Thank you for protecting my father, Captain. I'm grateful to the gods you are with him."

"The credit is not mine, Princess, but the honor of your trust I shall accept as always." His eyes crinkle. "Your father very clearly asked me on our way back to say to you that he is not in pain, which means he is, but you should not be asking about it."

Lira huffs. "That's what he says every time he nearly gets stabbed. He never learns. Neither do you."

Mion laughs quietly, then sobers. "We were ambushed halfway up the ridge. Would have all been ash if not for the mountain warrior."

"Nogas," I say, the name strange on my tongue. "Who is he, truly?"

Mion's gaze turns thoughtful. "He's Kalisidlan-born, an orphan raised by Chieftain Bantawan himself. Their tribe fights like stone turned to flame—and he is the best of them. They say the mountain itself listens when he strikes."

Lira snorts. "Men always sound grander in stories."

"Not this one, my love," says Mion. "For someone so young, he fights as if he's already seen the end of things. No wasted motion. No hesitation. Even the Datu watched him like he wasn't sure whether to thank him. Or fear him."

That image unsettles me more than I expect. "And now he's to guard me."

Lira lifts her chin. "Which means you can finally leave the palace walls without a council of old men breathing down your neck."

Mion nods in agreement. "He'll be loyal, Princess. I saw it in him. He didn't ask for reward or rest. He just helped us reach the mountain village. Had the Datu not asked for him, that young man would have disappeared right back into the shadows from where he came."

Their words weave together, steady and practical, until my anger thins into something else.

Resolve.

"Very well," I say at last. "If this is to be done, it will be done properly."

Lira and Mion exchange wary glances.

"Mion," I continue, my voice controlled now, the one my father trained me to use when giving orders. "See that Nogas is issued new armor in Hamtic steel, and a spear from the royal armory. He is to wear the sigil of my house on his clothing."

Mion bows. "It will be done, Princess."

"Tell him he begins service at dawn tomorrow. But have him meet me in my library, unarmed, once he has settled in the palace grounds."

Lira raises a brow. "Testing him already?"

I smile thinly. "If he is to stand at my side, I'd like to know what kind of storm he brings with him."

Mion inclines his head once more, then leaves to see it done.

When we are alone again, Lira watches me quietly. "You've changed your mind."

"No," I answer. "I have chosen my battlefield."

The breeze rustles through the garden, carrying the scent of wet stone and leaves. It feels like mountain air, somehow finding its way into the valley.

As I stand beneath the trees, I realize that whatever force has set this path in motion—light, omen, or fate—it has already begun to move us all.

CHAPTER 6

NOGAS

THE CAPTAIN OF THE ROYAL GUARD DOESN'T KNOCK on the door of my hut in the princess' palace grounds. Mion just pushes the door open and nods for me to stand.

"She has sent for you," he says without preamble. His voice carries that weary tone soldiers use when they have seen too much. "The princess wants to meet her new shadow."

I secure my belt and glance down at the unfamiliar silk tunic. It doesn't belong on me. The fabric is too fine, the scent too clean.

He chuckles at my discomfort. "You look half-strangled by civility. You'll get used to it."

"I doubt that, Captain," I say.

He snorts. "Don't tell the princess that. She was already fuming when she found out her father gave her a bodyguard.

You'll be lucky if she doesn't slice your throat with one of her scrolls."

"That would be a first," I murmur. "Dying by paper and ink."

He grins, but the humor fades quickly. "Listen to me, boy. She's more than she looks. The people love her, the court fears her, and her father…he's losing his grip on both. So mind your words, mind your eyes, and mind your heart. You'll need all three."

I nod once. "I understand."

"Good. Report to me at the royal barracks once you are done. We have much to do before the day is over."

Mion steps aside, and that's when a woman enters—swift as the wind, with eyes that miss nothing. She is wearing the same dark brown robes as the others working in the royal household, but lined with what looks to be silver thread.

"So this is him?" she asks, voice like a whip, her gaze raking over me from foot to forehead. "The mountain warrior who saved my fool husband?"

Mion winces. "Lira…"

She waves him off. "Did you know *someone* made my life miserable for days because they thought fighting raiders with half a squad was a good idea? If not for this boy, you would be dead, Mion. *Dead.* Do you even know what that means?"

I bow slightly. "Then I apologize, Lady. I didn't plan the ambush. Neither did I make any decisions for the captain."

She pauses, huffing a little. "At least you have a tongue. I thought you were all stone and silence."

"Stone listens," I reply. "It doesn't interrupt."

That earns the faintest smile. "I like this one. The palace has enough men who like the sound of their own voices."

Mion grunts, shaking his head, but he doesn't argue.

Lira tilts her head toward the doorway. "Come on. She's waiting."

The princess is seated inside a hut further down the grounds, one that's open to the sea breeze.

From the sight of scrolls and tablets stacked against the walls, it looks to be her library. Light spills through the woven panels, painting her skin in shifting gold. She sits behind a low table, a scroll in her hands.

Her light-colored robes are barely adorned, unlike the Datu's, but they are lined with gold thread that glints in the late afternoon sun. Her long, thick hair falls loosely around her softly rounded face, brows furrowed slightly as she reads.

When she looks up, the air forgets to move. Her eyes remind me of the first light of dawn breaking through the mist of the mountains.

"Princess," Lira says formally, bowing. "Nogas of the Kalisidlan, protector of the northern ridge. And now your shield."

Anini's gaze settles on me, steady and appraising. "I heard tell you saved my father and my people single-handedly."

I bow low. "Honor and duty demanded I intervene, Princess. I only did what was right at the time."

"Many say that," she replies softly. "Few mean it."

There's something in her eyes. Curiosity. Or warning. Perhaps both.

"Leave us, Lira," she says without looking away.

The older woman hesitates, glances at me once, then exits. The mats fall behind her, and the silence between us grows thick.

Anini sets down the scroll and leans back. "You don't seem like a man who enjoys courts."

"I don't, Princess," I admit. "Stone halls feel too small after mountains."

"Then why agree to this?"

"It was a request from Datu Oyong himself. Our tribe knows it is something that cannot be refused."

Her lips curve faintly. "And now here you stand, because someone could not say no."

"I was told when the river and the sun meet, they change the world," I say, choosing my words carefully. "Perhaps it is time Kalisidlan does not merely hide behind its fog and fires, Princess, but to flow where fate takes us next."

She studies me, the faintest spark of interest in her gaze. "You speak like a poet."

"I am a soldier," I answer. "We just learn to see things differently."

Her laughter is soft, startled from her before she can stop it. The sound makes my heart thrash against my chest.

She folds her hands. "My father tells me you'll serve as my shield. Do you understand what that means?"

"I'll guard you from threat, Princess."

"Good. But it's not only your blade that matters. It's your

presence. The court watches everything. The way you move, breathe, even where your eyes linger."

"I can control where I look," I say quietly.

"Can you?" she asks, tilting her head. "Then look at me now."

I do.

The space between us seems to hum. Her perfume is faint, reminding me of jasmine and herbs, but beneath it there's something stronger, like ink and rain. Her gaze holds mine, unflinching. The silence stretches until I feel it echo in my bones.

She finally blinks, breathing deeply. "You're not afraid."

"Should I be?"

"Most men are."

"I've seen worse than beauty."

Her breath catches, softly, but I notice. Then she rises, every movement slow, almost careful. She barely stands to my shoulder, but she carries herself with undeniable grace. The sunlight slides over her wrist as she passes, and her silken sleeve grazes my arm.

The contact is nothing.

But the effect is everything.

"You will begin tomorrow," she says, pausing at the doorway. "At dawn. I will be visiting the temple by the river to bring scrolls I have gathered from other kingdoms. We might as well conduct the rites of servitude there. The river shaman used to be my tutor."

I bow again. "As you command, Princess."

She lingers a moment, her silhouette framed by the afternoon light. Then, without another word, she leaves.

The moment she's gone, the tension snaps like a bowstring. I breathe again, unsteady, the scent of jasmine still clinging to me.

Mion warned me to mind my eyes.

He didn't warn me what it would feel like to be seen.

And as the woven mats sway in her wake, I realize something dangerous has begun.

Something quiet as breath, but unstoppable as the tide.

CHAPTER 7

Dream of Silence

Anini

T HE DREAM FEELS LIKE DROWNING.
The river meets the sun in blinding gold, and, for one impossible instant, they kiss.
Water and fire. Light and shadow.
And then…
Everything breaks.
The sky cracks open. The sea boils. I hear screams that are not mine, and then silence so vast it swallows the world.
I wake gasping.
My heart beats too fast, my skin drenched with sweat. The air in my hut feels too close, too thick to breathe. I push the blanket aside, my hands trembling.
Just a dream.
Only a dream.
But the heaviness in my chest won't fade.

I grab my shawl, drape it over my shift, and step into the night. The air is biting, restless. The torches have burned low, their smoke rising like ghosts. I walk barefoot through the courtyard, following the path of white stone until the cliffs open before me.

The sea below is silver against the night, the waves gliding against the rocks that look like sleeping beasts. I breathe in deep, pulling the scent of salt into my chest, and close my eyes.

"Princess."

The voice is quiet but unmistakable.

I turn. Nogas stands in the shadows near the cliff's edge. Bare-chested, hair loose, moonlight catching on the faint bronze clasp of my sigil at his throat.

"You shouldn't follow me," I say, trying to sound steady.

"I wasn't, Princess." His tone is even, unhurried. "I couldn't sleep."

I arch a brow. "The entire palace is yours to roam, yet you find yourself here?"

He steps closer, the wind tugging at his hair. "Seems we share poor timing."

"Coincidence?"

"Perhaps fate," he says simply.

I roll my eyes, but it does nothing to stop the pulse rising in my throat. "Do all mountain men flirt with omens?"

"Only when they walk into one."

Before I can reply, the night wind catches my shawl and pulls it loose. I reach to hold it, but Nogas moves first. He slips out of his own heavier cloak and places it gently over my shoulders.

"Wear this," he murmurs. "Yours won't be enough."

It's warm from his skin. The weave is thicker and rougher than Tinigbasan's fabrics, carrying the faint scent of leaves and metal.

"I didn't ask for it," I say, though I don't move to take it off.

"You also didn't ask to be guarded," he says. "But here I am. And I believe you need this cloak more than I do."

The corner of my mouth tilts. "You're persistent."

"Only with those worth guarding."

The silence stretches, fragile and charged. The sea hisses below. I look away first, out toward the horizon.

"I dreamt of fire," I say softly. "Of the river and the sun meeting. And then the world ending."

He glances at me. "Dreams remember what the waking try to forget."

"You sound like a shaman."

"No." His voice lowers. "Just someone who's seen too many endings."

Something about that makes my throat tighten. "And what about beginnings?"

He studies the sea. "They cost more, Princess. Just as this one did."

We stand side by side for a long time, saying nothing. The wind wraps around us, lifting the edges of his cloak that now clings to my shoulders. I can feel his warmth even from a step away.

"I don't like being guarded," I say eventually.

"I know."

"You'll do it anyway."

"Yes."

"Because you have been ordered to?"

"No." He turns to look at me fully now, eyes dark and steady. "Because now…I want to."

The words hang there, heavier than the night air.

My breath catches. "That sounds dangerously close to disobedience."

He gives the faintest smile. "I have faced worse dangers, Princess. Perhaps this time the danger might be worth facing."

For a heartbeat, the world feels too still. My pulse echoes the rhythm of the waves below. I can't tell whether I want to step closer.

Or to run.

"You should find somewhere else to walk," I say quietly. "Before someone thinks the mountain flame has burned the river's daughter."

He inclines his head. "Then perhaps I will stand farther. We both know I cannot stay away."

But he doesn't move.

The silence settles again, gentler this time. The moon climbs higher. Somewhere far below, the tide whispers against the rocks.

After what feels like forever, I sigh. "I should go back."

"I'll walk you."

"You don't have to."

"I know," he says again, but he follows.

When we reach the path leading back to my hut, I stop and turn. "You can take your cloak."

He shakes his head. "Keep it. The wind hasn't changed yet. I doubt it will soon."

Our eyes meet again, and something unspoken passes between us.

Something I don't dare name.

"Goodnight, Nogas."

"Goodnight, Princess."

He waits until I'm inside before he turns away.

I sit on my sleeping mats, still wrapped in his cloak. It's too warm, too heavy, too full of him.

But I pull it tighter around me.

When I finally close my eyes, the river and the sun meet again.

This time, the world doesn't break.

It just burns.

CHAPTER 8

Dark of Dawn

Nogas

Before sunrise, the cliffs remain halfway in the dark.

I look at the Tinigbasan peaks painted at the edges with thin blue light, breathing in the scents of salt and dew. The sea beneath looks black and endless. I finish my training where the stone meets the air, sweat cutting down my back.

But I remain steady against the wind. Against everything that is changing right before my eyes.

The spear in my hands arcs through mist, the blade singing softly as it cleaves the air. Each movement flows into the next.

Strike. Pivot. Turn.

This is how I pray.

In the mountains, we don't kneel to gods. We kneel to the earth, the wind, the quiet pulse beneath the stone.

Mion's words still echo in my head. After meeting the princess yesterday, the captain took me around the palaces and grounds, and gave a long talk about the duties of a royal shield.

"A hundred paces, no farther. You are her breath, her shadow. She moves, you move."

I don't know what to make of it. In the northern ridge, my hut stood alone. I built it with my own hands, a wall of wood and silence between me and the world. When I left the chieftain's household, I told myself solitude was discipline. That quiet was strength.

But here, quiet feels like waiting.

The first edge of sunlight spills over the sea. My routine should be simple: train before dawn, eat before sunrise, stand ready when the princess wakes.

A rhythm. A rule. I should be used to that.

But nothing about this feels the same.

I bathe in cold water from the basin beside my hut. The chill bites my skin, clears my thoughts. Then I dress quickly, as I always do.

The dark brown tunic lined with gold thread fits too closely. The silk feels like it belongs to someone else. I put on the light armor of the Tinigbasan Royal Guard, its thin metal whispering when I move.

Anini's sigil, a fish tail, gleams in the bronze clasp at my collar. It's smaller and more distinct, compared to the Datu's tree. But it suits her. Power hidden behind grace.

I strap on my daggers. Seven of them, balanced in their familiar places at my belt, around my calf, and in my bracers. I take my spear last, the one from home, carved from northern wood and marked with sun-cycles of use. The new one Mion chose for me sits untouched in the corner. It's too polished. Too proud.

When I step out, the horizon burns gold.

The princess is already there.

Anini stands in the courtyard, her back to me, her robe the color of pearl in the new light. Her hair glows faintly, haloed by the dawn. For a moment, I almost forget to breathe.

"You're late," she says without turning.

I stop behind her. "I'm not."

"You are," she replies, voice calm but laced with challenge. "The sun is up. I rise before it. You should have been here already."

My mouth quirks, unbidden. "Would you rather I watch you sleep, Princess? So I never miss the moment you wake?"

That gets her attention. She turns, brows arching, and for an instant I see the smile she's trying not to show.

"Perhaps someday," she says, eyes gleaming. "But you have yet to earn the right to be close."

I bow slightly. "You are not like your father. You trust far less than he does."

Her gaze flickers. "No. I'm not. You'll learn that soon enough."

"I already have."

She studies me for a heartbeat, long enough that I feel the weight of it. "You're bold."

"Not bold, Princess," I say evenly. "Just honest."

Her lips curve faintly. "Then honesty will be your test."

"I thought I was here to fight."

"Fighting is the easy part." She takes a step closer, the

sunlight catching in her eyes. "If you want to be my shadow, you'll have to earn it. You'll have to prove yourself."

"Prove myself how?"

Her gaze holds mine, unwavering. "You fight for it. You fight for me."

Her words hang in the air between us, steady and certain. I swallow before answering.

"Are you asking if I'm ready, Princess?"

"I'm asking if you *want* to be."

I meet her eyes. "Yes, Princess. I do."

Her smile this time is real. Dangerously so. "We'll see."

She turns, her robe whispering over the stone. "Come. We're late for breakfast."

"Will you not be eating in your palace?" I ask as I fall in beside her.

"No. I eat with my people."

We walk along the stone path toward the royal commons, the morning brightening around us. Her pace is graceful. I move forward slightly, taking the lead as protocol demands, and she notices.

"You remember the rule, then," she says lightly.

"I remember what I was told, Princess."

"And what do *you* believe?"

"That I should walk where the danger comes first."

She hums softly. "And what if the danger walks beside you?"

"Then I shall keep pace."

For a long stretch, there's only the sound of our footsteps.

Then she says, almost to herself, "I didn't sleep well last night."

"Because of what happened to your father?" I ask. "Or your…dream?"

"Perhaps both," she says quietly. "Or something else entirely."

"What else?"

"Having you here feels…different. I can't explain it."

I swallow hard, my fingers digging into my palms. The spear feels heavy and cold on my back. "You're not alone in that."

"Oh?"

"This feels different to me, too," I admit. "Everything does. Even the light."

"The light?"

"It looks new, Princess," I say. "As if it is touching the world for the first time."

"Maybe it is."

We walk in silence again until the path narrows, the hall now in sight.

I pause, lowering my head toward her. "Princess, you will have to teach me how to serve you. I don't know the ways of courts."

She stops walking, then nods faintly. "Don't expect kindness if you falter."

"I never do."

A faint smile ghosts across her face before it fades.

I bow, then turn toward the path to the hall, stepping before her once more.

"Nogas," she says. "Stop."

I turn back to her. "Yes, Princess?"

"I'll ask one thing of you, as my shield."

"What is that?"

Her voice is unwavering, her tone direct. "Look at me."

I raise my eyes to hers.

The morning light gilds her face, her hair catching the wind. For a moment, she doesn't look like royalty. She looks like something alive and untamed, something the sea itself would bow to.

"Always tell me the truth," she says. "Even when it's something I don't want to hear. *Especially* when it's something I don't want to hear."

I pause, searching her eyes. "The truth, Princess?"

"Yes. That's how you'll serve me. With truth."

My throat feels dry. "What truth do you wish me to speak now?"

She hesitates, then says quietly, "Tell me what you see in this new light you speak of."

For a moment, words fail me. Then they don't.

"Something worth burning for," I say.

Her breath catches. She doesn't say anything in response.

Instead, she walks past me. This time, her shoulder brushes my arm. I feel the silk of her robes and her skin. The warmth of her.

It feels like being struck.

But I follow her in silence.

The morning sun has broken fully now. Below the cliffs, the river glitters, the air heavy with golden light.

All I can think is that I've already begun to burn.

CHAPTER 9

Promise of the Sea

Anini

The morning spills gold over the thatched rooftops of Tinigbasan.

By the time Nogas and I enter the common hall, the court is already alive with chatter. The air smells of rice cakes and roasted fish, of coconut milk simmering in clay pots. My people bow as I pass, their smiles warm, their eyes curious. I feel the weight of every glance settle on the man at my shoulder.

The mountain warrior.

My new shadow.

The long tables are lined with the familiar faces of stewards, guards, and handmaidens. Clay cups clink softly. Steam rises from banana leaves, and the air fills with quiet laughter. I've sat here every morning since I was old enough to hold a cup steady, but today feels different. Today, there's him.

Nogas follows a few steps behind me, his movements precise but unhurried. Even the guards lower their voices when he enters. His presence charges the air in ways I can't name.

I stop beside the main table and glance at him.

"You'll sit there," I say, gesturing toward the long bench where the royal guards dine.

He bows low. "Princess, I—"

"It's not a request." My tone is soft but leaves no room for question. "You eat with them. You're one of them now."

He hesitates, just for a breath, then inclines his head. "As you command."

As he moves toward the table, the guards straighten instinctively. Their talk falters.

Around me, I catch fragments of low whispers.

"They say he does not fight like a man," someone murmurs.

"Lightning, said my brother. He was there."

"Did you see his spear?" another adds. "What's it made of?"

"He doesn't even look at anyone…"

"Maybe he doesn't need to."

I turn away before my mouth betrays a smile.

My seat is at the other end of the hall, where the court ladies and noble maidens gather. They rise when I approach, silks rustling, jewels glinting. They all bow slightly, eyes gleaming with curiosity, voices sharp and thick as melted sugar.

"Princess Anini," one of them sings, "your new shield has the hall talking already."

"Is it true he fought off an entire horde of raiders alone?" another asks.

"I heard more," someone else whispers loudly. "That his tribe uses sunlight as a weapon. That he blinded the whole enemy line."

I pour myself a cup of warm tea, letting their chatter weave around me.

"People do love their stories," I say lightly.

"But you've seen him, haven't you?" asks one of the younger maidens, her tone conspiratorial. "Up close?"

I glance toward the guards' table. Nogas sits among them but apart, his posture still and straight, eyes lowered. He eats in silence, seemingly oblivious to every stare. The sun catches in his hair, glinting like a blade edge.

"I have seen him," I answer. "He is…disciplined."

"Disciplined," one echoes, her eyes sparkling. "That's one word for it."

A ripple of laughter passes through the group.

"He doesn't even look at anyone," another sighs. "If he's your shield, Princess, does he ever look at you?"

I sip my tea slowly. "When he needs to."

For a moment, even I am startled by my tone, but I don't dwell on it.

"I don't need him to look at me," says another maiden. "He can stay in front of or behind me all he wants."

Gasps and giggles rise from the table. Someone fans herself dramatically.

"Careful," an older lady chides, smiling behind her sleeve.

"If the Datu hears you say that, he'll have you sweeping stables for impertinence."

"Then perhaps the stables will be well-guarded," the maiden shoots back, earning more laughter.

I let their mirth ripple through the air, their teasing turning the hall bright and warm. The meal continues in its usual rhythm. I partake of grilled fish wrapped in pandan leaves, mango slices dusted with salt, and ginger broth poured steaming into earthen cups. I eat as custom dictates, slowly and gracefully, but my thoughts drift.

The unease brought about by my vision at the river and last night's dream sits in my chest, heavy and restless. When a steward bends low and murmurs that my father summons me, I almost feel relief.

"Please let Lira know," I tell the women. "She will be with her son and Mion at this time. Once she is ready, tell her to get my caravan to wait in the courtyard for the journey to the temple. We shall depart before the sun climbs high."

Nogas is already on his feet before I reach the door. His timing is unnervingly precise. I don't ask how he knew. The murmurs in the hall follow us out.

He falls into step beside me as we cross the courtyard, the early light warming the stones. The Datu's palace looms ahead, tall and imposing, carved beams gleaming like the roots of the mountain itself.

When we enter, my father stands near the window in his hall, speaking quietly with two advisors. At the sight of us, he dismisses them with a wave. They bow to him, then to me.

I bow before him. "Good morning, Father. You summoned me."

"Leave us," he says to the guards in the room, then turns to Nogas. "You too."

Nogas bows and obeys without hesitation, following the others as they retreat quietly from the hall.

I turn back to my father. The light through the shutters paints his face in gold and shadow. There's a map unfurled on the table beside him, weighed down with stones, its edges curling from wear.

"Come, Anini," he says, gesturing to the low tables. "Sit."

I do. My heart feels heavier than the silence that follows.

He joins me, then studies me for a long while before speaking. "You have seen your new guardian in daylight now. What do you think of him?"

"He's…capable," I say carefully. "Quiet. Loyal."

"Loyal?" My father's brow furrows. "A man who kills with that kind of precision is loyal only to his blade."

"Perhaps," I reply softly. "But his blade saved your life."

He breathes out slowly, eyes dropping to the map. "Yes. And now that blade belongs to you."

There's something behind his tone, something tight and uncertain. "Father, what's troubling you?"

He doesn't look at me. "This morning, I received word from Dalidnon."

My breath catches. "Dalidnon?"

"The seafaring kingdom," he says. "Datu Radul and his son, Prince Sidlaw. They intend to visit Tinigbasan in a few days' time, earlier if the tide is in their favor. They heard of what happened in the mountains and wish to offer protection."

I almost laugh, but it comes out as a sigh. "Protection."

His eyes lift to mine. "They wish for alliance."

"Alliance," I repeat. "With their ships. With their armies. With their—"

"Blood," he finishes quietly.

The word hangs there, heavy and cutting.

I swallow. "Sidlaw."

I remember him, tall and strapping, bronze-skinned and proud. He had the sea's confidence and twice its arrogance. Even as a child, I'd known to dislike him.

He had once called me *little river* as if it were a compliment. I had wanted to throw him into one.

My father watches me closely. "He's grown into a fine man. A prince of the sea. A true warrior of the tides. Datu Radul believes the sea should embrace the river."

"I know what you mean, Father." My voice is calm. My pulse is not. "I know exactly what you mean."

He meets my eyes steadily. "Sidlaw is your best match, Anini. You know this."

"I know he's arrogant. And believes all should be grateful to look his way."

My father's lips tighten. "You speak like your mother. Always sharp when frightened."

"I'm not frightened," I answer tightly.

"Yes, you are. So am I." He stands up and walks toward the window, staring out at the far horizon where the river meets the sea.

"Tinigbasan grows weaker by the day. We don't have the ships, the reach, the numbers. We don't have the gold. The raiders become more daring. If the Dalidnon stand with us, we can hold the borders. Without them…"

"They think I am weak," he finishes heavily, reaching up to rub his temples slowly.

"You're not," I say.

"Perhaps I am," he admits. "I am not a warrior like my father or his before him. But I am a statesman. I can feel when a kingdom trembles. If the Dumalog are bold enough to strike in Kalisidlan, what stops them from attacking Tinigbasan next?"

"Then speak with them as a statesman," I urge, getting to my feet to stand next to him. "Speak with them as someone who cares for his kingdom, not just war."

"We have tried," he says bitterly. "And my older brother, the rightful Datu, lost his head for it. They cut him down in the water. The Dumalog are no longer pirates. They are something else now. They want our rivers, our crops, our children's soil."

The air leaves my lungs.

"The Dumalog have always envied the mainland," he continues, voice low and taut. "They want to abandon their dead islands and claim our lands. For generations they have threatened, but now they move differently. They are smarter now. More organized. They know our trade routes, our defenses. They want to destroy what we are at the root."

The words leave me in a shaky whisper. "At the river's heart."

He nods grimly. "If Dalidnon stands with us, they'll think twice. If Sidlaw stands beside you, no one will dare raise a blade against Tinigbasan. You will be untouchable."

His voice breaks slightly, and something inside me folds in on itself.

The word tastes like ash as I say it. "Untouchable."

"Yes," he says, relief evident in his voice. "No one would dare harm the Jewel of Hamtic if she becomes the Dayang of Dalidnon. The river and the sea, united. Finally."

He turns to me, smiling faintly. "Perhaps, my daughter, we could finally know peace."

Peace. At the cost of myself.

I don't answer at first. I watch the light trace across his hair, the same gray as the dawn clouds. A lump rises in my throat.

At last, I manage, "I understand what you mean, Father. I understand what you want."

He exhales, shoulders loosening. "I knew you would. You have your mother's wisdom. Her courage."

He draws me into an embrace. His scent is of old sandalwood and worry.

"Go," he says gently. "To the temple. Bring your scrolls. Complete your rites. I have asked Mion to select the ten best men of the Royal Guard for your caravan. And with that Kalisidlan warrior beside you, the raiders will think twice before striking again."

I pull back slightly. "His name is Nogas."

He blinks. "What?"

"His name," I repeat. "It's Nogas. And he is not a warrior. He's my shield."

"Of course," my father says after a pause, the confusion flickering just long enough to show. "Of course, my daughter."

I bow low. "By your leave, Datu."

When I straighten, the world feels smaller.

And when I turn, the tears fall before I can stop them. Quiet and unbidden, breaking loose from inside me.

Outside, the morning light feels harsher.

Nogas stands at the far end of the courtyard, still and straight as a spear, his shadow long across the stones. For a heartbeat, our eyes meet.

I know he sees me breaking.

I turn away and walk in the opposite direction, my tears slipping silently down my cheeks.

His footsteps follow, patient and restrained. I can't see him but I feel him, the echo of a promise I never asked for.

For the first time, I wonder what it truly means to have a shield.

And who it is meant to protect.

CHAPTER 10

Shield of Truth

Nogas

THE WIND MOVES SOFTLY THROUGH THE COURTYARD, but no one speaks to me when we step out.

I remain outside the Datu's hall, waiting. The guards stand at attention nearby, their voices low.

I can hear the muffled rhythm of conversation behind the carved doors, her voice faint and the Datu's deeper, measured tones.

The air feels like something rippling beneath sand and stone. Every few breaths, my fingers tighten around the haft of my spear.

"She's with him a while," one of the younger guards murmurs.

Another snorts. "If Dalidnon's message is true, it's no wonder. Their prince is coming here himself."

"Sidlaw?" someone asks. "I last saw him many cycles ago, when he was just a boy."

"Yes. Now he's a man grown, with golden ships and half the ocean in his pocket. With our princess in his sights!"

They chuckle softly, the sound like grit underfoot.

"Imagine that," says another. "Our Jewel of Hamtic, soon to be the Dayang of Dalidnon. The river marries the sea."

"And its army," adds someone else. "Our Datu knows what he's doing."

The words are careless, but something cuts through me.

I don't understand it at first.

It isn't anger. Not exactly. It isn't envy either.

It's a tightening, low and deep, the feeling of ropes and vines pulled too tight around my chest. I tell myself it means nothing, that she is a princess and I am her shield, but the thought twists and clings.

"Dalidnon's prince will bring his ships, his soldiers," one of them adds knowingly, "and perhaps take her away in exchange."

Take her away.

I force myself to take slow, steady breaths. The spear's wood creaks under my grip.

The doors open, then she steps out.

Anini moves like sunlight, quiet but blinding. Her face is composed, but her eyes...

Her eyes are rimmed in red, as if she's been staring at the horizon too long.

For a moment, our gazes meet. It's only a flicker, then she turns away.

She walks in the opposite direction without a word.

I follow. Not close enough to offend, not far enough to lose sight. I keep to about twenty paces. The measured distance of a guard, a shadow.

She takes the narrow path that skirts the palace cliffs, her robe trailing dust across the stones. The air grows cooler as we climb, and the sound of the sea swells below us.

At the top, she stops beneath a cluster of trees, their branches dripping with dew. From here, the whole kingdom lies below. I can see the terraces, the river, and the far curve of the ocean where sky and water meet.

This was where she found me last night.

She doesn't turn, but I know she knows I'm there. I keep my distance at first, standing half in shadow.

The wind pulls at her hair. She's been crying. She hides it well, but I can see it in the small movements. The way she wipes her face without thought, the way her shoulders sink slightly as if she is carrying something heavy.

The sun climbs higher, spilling through the canopy. Its glare hits her eyes, and before I think, I move.

I walk to her side and stand beside her, close enough that my shadow falls over her face.

She doesn't flinch. She doesn't thank me.

She only says, softly, "Tell me something true, Nogas."

I glance at her. "True, Princess?"

"Yes." Her voice is so quiet the wind almost carries it away. "A secret. Something you would never tell anyone. Or something you would tell a stranger if you knew you will never see them again."

For a long time, I say nothing. The waves crash below, distant and steady.

Finally, I answer, "I have only known war, Princess. Fighting. All my life, they told me I was a warrior, that I was built for battle. And I believed them."

Her eyes find mine. "Your family told you this?"

I shake my head. "I never knew them, Princess. I have no one. The chief of Kalisidlan raised me himself. Bantawan had sons and daughters of his own, but I was his weapon. His blade. I was told my parents were killed by another tribe before I could even speak. Perhaps that's why it was easy for him to let me go when your father asked for tribute."

Anini looks back toward the sea. The light flickers over her face, turning her tears to gold.

"It's easy to make the choice, isn't it?" she murmurs. "To sacrifice one for peace. For the good of many."

"There are those who make the choices," I say softly, "and those who live with them."

Her voice hardens a little. "What would you have chosen, Nogas?"

I think for a moment. The truth tastes strange in my mouth. "I would have asked you what you wanted, Princess."

Her head tilts, eyes narrowing slightly. "What I wanted?"

"Yes. Whether you wanted a shield, or a blade."

She breathes out, the faintest laugh breaking through. "Or a cage."

I meet her gaze. "Or a cage."

Her eyes drop to the ground. "It was never my choice to make."

"What if it was?" I ask. "What if you had a choice?"

She smiles faintly, but there's no warmth in it. "I don't know. It would never have happened anyway."

"If it does," I say, "will you honor me with the truth? When the choice comes, whatever it is?"

She looks up again, her expression distant, almost as if she is trying to keep the pain away. "If only it were that easy."

I allow myself a small smile. "Having a choice is never easy, Princess. Perhaps that's why so few are chosen to make them. And fewer still can bear what comes after."

Silence stretches between us. The wind sighs through the trees.

Anini wipes away her tears once more, taking deep breaths.

Then I hear footsteps.

Lira appears from the path, her voice gentle. "I knew I'd find you here."

There's a knowing look between Anini and the older woman. The kind that carries more words than it says.

"Is the princess ready to depart?" Lira asks softly.

"She is," I answer before Anini can.

Anini glances at me, then nods. "Yes. Let's go."

We descend the path together, the sea at our backs, the air growing warmer with each step.

At the foot of the cliffs, the caravan awaits. There are three maidens, ten guards, and two carriages pulled by great water beasts whose hides shimmer like oil under the sun. Servants bustle about, loading provisions, tightening straps.

Datu Oyong stands beside the bigger carriage, Captain Mion at his shoulder. The Datu's face is pale, his movements slower than yesterday.

"I would have gone with you," he says, his voice strained, "but the healers ordered against it."

Anini takes his hand and bows her head. "You have done enough, Father. Rest."

Mion steps forward, his arm in a sling but his posture still proud. "I'll see to the Datu myself, Princess. You have my word."

She grips his uninjured arm. "And you'll report to me directly on my father, Captain. No delays."

Mion smiles faintly. "As always, Princess. You have my word."

They speak a little longer, exchanging promises of caution, prayer, and trust. Then Anini steps into her carriage, lifting her chin high though I can see the strain in her eyes.

I take my place next to the carriage, right at her side, the spear in my hand glinting faintly in the sun. When the caravan begins to move, the beasts' hooves beat against the earth like drums.

Behind us, the Datu stands watching, one hand raised in farewell, his robes waving in the breeze.

Ahead, the road curves toward the temple, toward whatever choice waits there.

Beside her carriage, I walk—her shadow, her silence, her shield—and wonder which one she will need most.

CHAPTER 11

Serpent of the Hill

ANINI

T HE PATH DOWN FROM THE PEAK WINDS LIKE A serpent through mist and rock.

It takes half a day to reach the temple, sometimes longer if the rain falls early. Today, the air feels still. Above, the sky is colorless, the kind of gray that feels like a warning.

We ride without fanfare and little noise. The sound of the water beasts pulling the carriages is steady, their hooves thudding against the damp earth.

Nogas walks beside mine.

Always within sight. Always silent.

I can see him when I glance through the small window. I see the easy rhythm of his stride, the spear balanced across his back, the way he moves with the wind like he belongs to it.

"You didn't bring the spear from the royal armory," I tell him, just to make sure he still speaks.

"No, Princess," he answers. "I prefer my own weapons. In Kalisidlan, each weapon is forged for the warrior bearing it. No two blades are the same."

I incline my head at the daggers strapped to his belt. "Not even those?"

He follows my gaze, then shakes his head. "They were forged at different times of my life. The first when I won my warrior rites at age ten. The others to honor victories in the tribe."

By midday, we stop beneath a grove to eat. Dried fish and rice wrapped in leaves, with a little broth and tea. The guards stay on watch, and I eat quickly, listening to the wind rustle in the trees.

It's quiet. Too quiet.

When we resume, clouds gather low and dark above the canopy. The first thunder rolls far off, deep enough to rattle the carriages.

The beasts snort uneasily. Nogas murmurs instructions on navigating the road to one of the drivers, his voice almost lost under the rumble of the sky.

Then the rain begins.

Soft and gentle at first, scattered drops that melt into the dust. Then it pours louder, harder, until the sound becomes a roar.

The path turns slick. Water spills down the stones in silver threads. The carriages groan as the beasts struggle to keep balance.

I look out the window, shielding my eyes from the downpour with my sleeve. Everything is a blur of color.

Branches bend under the weight of water, leaves shudder, the paths begin to run dark and turn to mud.

But it's not the storm that makes my heart quicken.

It's the silence between the thunder.

The birds have gone quiet.

Even the wind is nowhere to be heard.

Nogas stops walking. I see him turn quickly, his head tilting, his hand gripping his spear.

Something changes in his posture. He freezes, becoming utterly still.

Then his voice cuts through the rain.

"PRINCESS! DOWN!"

The carriage door bursts open before I can react. He reaches in, grabs me by the waist, and yanks me into the rain.

Arrows hiss past us. One tears through the carriage window where my head was.

"We're under attack!" he roars. "Dumalog!"

Everything explodes.

The forest comes alive with movement. Men leap from the trees. Their bodies are streaked with mud and moss, faces painted in brown and green. They blend into the trunks, into the earth itself. Blades flash. Arrows rain down.

The first beast shrieks as a shaft pierces its throat. The second collapses in the mud, dragging the carriage sideways. The guards scramble, shields up, forming a line.

"Defend the princess!" one shouts, but the rain swallows the words.

I stumble, soaked, the world spinning in flashes of

silver and red. Nogas pushes me behind him, his voice steady and terrifyingly calm.

"Stay low."

Then he moves.

I have seen men fight. But never like this.

Nogas becomes a storm given form.

He lunges forward, his spear cutting through the rain with a hiss. The blade catches the lightning, bright and blinding, and then the first raider falls.

The second swings. Nogas sidesteps, then grabs his wrist, breaking it with a twist. He drives the butt of his spear into the man's throat.

Two more charge. He spins the spear in a perfect arc, striking one across the ribs and impaling the other through the chest in one motion.

The guards rally behind him, shouting, their fear replaced with raw survival. One goes down, an arrow buried in his side. Another takes his place.

The air fills with the smell of iron and wet bark. The rain runs red.

A raider lunges from the side. I see him before Nogas does.

"Left!" I cry out.

He pivots instantly, slamming his elbow into the man's face, sending him sprawling into the mud.

But I can barely see anything at all. Just flashes before me—the gleam of the spear, the sharp turn of his body, the sound of bone cracking under impact. It's brutal and beautiful and terrible all at once.

And then another arrow sings toward me. Too close.

Nogas catches it midair, then snaps it in half.

That's when I realize if I do nothing, I'll be next.

"Princess!" he shouts. "Stay down!"

But I'm already moving.

I reach for his belt, fingers closing around two daggers, and before he can stop me, I'm gone.

I hear him curse furiously, but I don't look back.

The rain blinds me, but my body remembers. Every lesson Mion ever taught me in secret. Every movement practiced in the dark of my chamber, in the silence of the shadows.

The first raider swings low. I duck, slide under his arm, and drive the dagger into his thigh. He screams. I twist, using his own momentum to pull the blade free, turning into the next strike.

The second man grabs my wrist. I bring the hilt up hard into his jaw, spin, and then slash. Blood mixes with water, dark and steaming.

A third comes from behind. I step aside, let him overshoot, then bury the blade in my left hand to his side.

The forest is chaos. The rain deafening. But every motion feels clear. Every heartbeat a drum.

Someone grabs my cloak. I tear free, drop to one knee, and throw the dagger in my right hand. It hits the raider, clean in the chest.

"ANINI!"

Nogas reaches me just as another man lunges, intercepting him mid-step. He drives his spear straight through the man's stomach. The impact sends a spray of blood across my sleeve.

Now we're back-to-back.

Breathing hard. Surrounded.

The guards form a rough circle around the carriages. Lira and the maidens huddle inside, daggers trembling in their hands. One of the drivers is down. The other grips a short blade, teeth bared.

The enemy keeps coming.

Nogas twists his spear free. He reaches into his bracer and pulls out another dagger.

"You should not be fighting, Princess," he says as he tosses the blade to me.

I laugh breathlessly as I catch it by the hilt. The sound of my voice is wild, even to my own ears.

"Apparently, neither should you," I hiss at him.

Nogas only lowers his head, lips curving slightly.

We move as one when they charge.

His spear cuts wide arcs through the downpour, clearing space around us. I twist and strike fast where he leaves openings, quick and close. I aim for throats, ribs, wrists. The guards close ranks, driving the raiders back inch by inch.

The forest trembles with the violence of it.

The clash of steel. The screams. The splash and steam of rain on blood.

There is no thought. No fear. Only movement.

I feel the river in my veins, the pulse of the mountain in my breath.

"Stand your ground!" I cry out, voice hoarse. "No one runs!"

Nogas glances over his shoulder, eyes catching mine

through the curtain of rain. "I don't think you need a shield at all, Princess."

Lightning flashes, close enough to burn.

"No," I say, adjusting my grip around the daggers in my hands. "I needed a bigger blade for the world to see."

The storm rages on.

Together, we turn to face it.

CHAPTER 12

Rain of Fire

Nogas

T HE WORLD IS NOISE.

Rain. Blood. Metal. Breath.

Every sound folds into the next until there's only rhythm.

Strike. Step. Turn. Breathe.

The raiders press in from all sides, but the line holds. I plant my spear in the mud and drive it forward through the gap between shields, catching one of them under the ribs. He screams, choked and short, before collapsing into the muck. I pull free, turn, and bring the blade across another's neck.

Anini is beside me now, her movements swift and sure. I can hear the daggers cutting through rain and flesh.

"Stay behind me, Princess," I growl. "You're too open.

"I told you," she pants, ducking under a swinging axe. "I needed a bigger blade."

I don't know whether to curse or laugh.

So I fight.

A raider lunges at her from the flank. I grab her by the shoulder, twist her around behind me, and use her momentum to drive my spear through his stomach. She doesn't flinch. Instead, she steps around me, slicing clean across another's arm before he can raise his weapon.

We move like a single thing. Her motion feeds mine. Mine protects hers. Her breath is quick in my ear. My blood drums in my chest.

Every time she moves, the world narrows to the space between us.

I spin the spear low to sweep a man's legs out from under him. She vaults over the falling body, planting both her blades into the next attacker's chest. When he crumples, she lands lightly next to me, mud splattering her face and throat.

The sight of her, so fierce and alive, nearly knocks the breath from me.

Arrows sing overhead. I shove her down, throw my shoulder up to shield her as one clatters off my armor. She grips my arm, steadying herself. Her skin burns through the rain.

"Keep low," I bark, but she's already moving again.

The guards rally, forming a half-circle behind us. I hear one cry out in pain, another shouting for reinforcements to their side, and still another praying.

The maidens scream from the wrecked carriages.

"Princess," Lira shouts. "Princess, come back!"

But Anini doesn't listen.

She's in the storm now, and she won't retreat.

I pull her close for one brief breath, her shoulder pressed to my chest, and shove her toward the left flank. "There!"

She moves without hesitation. Together we break through, blades flashing in tandem. Every swing of my spear clears her path, every movement of hers draws an opening for mine.

She catches an enemy's wrist, twists, and drives her dagger into his throat.

I see the moment the blood sprays across her cheek, and her smile after. Not joy. Not triumph. Just fierce, merciless resolve.

Thunder rolls overhead. Lightning ignites the treetops in white fire.

For a heartbeat, I swear I can see her framed in that light, hair plastered to her skin, eyes burning bright.

And then the horns sound.

From below the ridge, a new wave of shouting rises.

Different voices this time. Men in armor surge from the forest, their weapons gleaming with coiled sigils. Their banners rise through the mist, green against gray.

"Princess, it's the Temple Guard!" Lira cries out.

Reinforcements.

The raiders hesitate. Then they panic.

The guards from the temple crash into them like a tide, cutting through their flanks, driving them back toward the ravine.

I seize the opening. "Push forward!"

Our remaining men roar in answer. In moments, the field changes completely.

The enemy scatters and falls, retreating into the trees.

And just like that, it's over.

The rain softens to a drizzle.

The mud underfoot is red. My lungs burn.

Anini is still gripping the daggers, chest rising and falling fast. She looks at the fallen, at the blood on her hands.

Then, without hesitation, she walks to me.

"Yours," she says, holding out both blades.

I reach for them, but she doesn't let go immediately. Her fingers brush mine, skin lingering on skin. I see the rain trail down her wrist, over her knuckles.

For a moment, neither of us moves.

Then she releases them, smiling faintly. "You fight well."

I bow my head. "But you burn brighter, Princess."

A laugh escapes her, soft and breathless. "That's dangerous talk."

"It's the truth."

Before she can answer, a figure strides toward us. Broad-shouldered, armor dented, his gray cloak torn. He bows deeply.

"Princess Anini," he says. "By the gods, you're alive."

"Captain Joru!" she exclaims, relief flooding her face. "You came from the temple?"

He nods grimly. "We were attacked as well. The Dumalog struck at dawn just before the sunrise prayers. Caught us off guard. The shaman and two scholars fell before we could rally. But we drove them back." His jaw tightens. "When the storm broke, I took half my men and followed the river road. I feared they'd come for you too."

Her expression hardens, the princess returning to the surface. "You were right."

Joru lowers his head. "I am very sorry about Shaman Agdan, Princess. He was the first to fall. But he did not suffer."

"I see," she says softly. I see the tremble in her lip, but everything else she carries with composure. "And where is he now?"

"At the banks, Princess."

"I would like to see him, Captain."

He nods, then glances around at the carnage, the broken carriages, the blood. Then his eyes settle on me. "And who's this?"

Anini steps closer to me, shoulders squared. "My shield. Nogas of Kalisidlan."

"The warrior of the northern peaks," Joru says. "I've heard of you. Of what you did for Datu Oyong."

"I wish it were under better circumstances, Captain," I reply.

He grunts. "Don't we all?"

The temple guards begin tending to the wounded and gathering supplies. One of the beasts is still alive, trembling in pain. The driver kneels beside it, whispering prayers.

Lira runs to Anini, tears streaming down her face. "Princess! You're hurt!"

"I'm fine," Anini says, wiping a streak of blood from her temple.

"Fine?" Lira's voice cracks. "You fought like—like one of them! You could have been killed!"

Anini takes her by the hands. "See, Lira? I told you. I needed this. All those hours, all those bruises. They kept me alive."

Lira shakes her head, laughing and crying at the same time. "You're impossible."

"I'm alive," Anini answers simply. "That's enough."

I can't help the smile that pulls at my mouth. She sees it, and her eyes narrow, but there's warmth in it.

I turn away and walk a few steps ahead as she tells Lira about Agdan. I can hear Lira sobbing, but I don't look back.

The temple men finish loading the dead and the wounded. Scrolls, supplies, and weapons are gathered, packed onto carts salvaged from the wreckage. The rain has nearly stopped now, leaving only steam rising from the blood-wet ground.

As we begin making our way to the last stretch of the path toward the river temple, Joru turns to us, his face grave.

"We managed to take one of the Dumalog alive," he says. "He's at the temple. Wounded, but breathing."

Anini's gaze narrows. "Have you questioned him?"

"We tried. He won't speak to anyone." Joru hesitates. "Except…"

She frowns. "Except who?"

Joru glances at me. "Except the mountain warrior, Princess. Your shield."

Anini turns to me slowly, realization dawning in her face. "They know you. They knew you were coming here."

The rain starts again, relentless in its steadiness.

For the first time, I feel cold.

CHAPTER 13

Anini

T HE RIVER TEMPLE SITS LOW AGAINST THE VALLEY, shattered in parts but still standing.

Its walls of reed and stone still hold, but the roof has fallen in places. Black smoke trails upward, a faint ribbon against the pale afternoon sky. The air carries the stench of burnt wood and wet ash.

We follow Joru down the slippery steps carved into the hillside. The path glistens from the rain.

When the temple comes fully into view, my chest tightens.

Stone pillars rise from the mud, carved with prayers in old script. Fragments of charms and broken oil lamps litter the ground. Scrolls lie half-buried under ash and debris.

Someone has tried to salvage what they could. Scattered

are bundles of parchment tied in reed fiber, clay jars rescued from the flames, and relics lined in neat rows.

Lira gasps softly, still shaky from the news about Agdan. "By the gods…"

Joru keeps walking ahead, leading the way. His armor is stained with soot and blood. "The bodies are by the bank, Princess. We prepare them for the sunset rites."

I nod. My voice feels lost somewhere behind my ribs.

The river glints through the trees, a long silver vein beneath the fading light. Smoke drifts low over the water.

We step into the clearing.

They have laid the dead in a line along the riverbank, each covered in a woven mat and flower garlands. I count nine in all. The scholars in their gray robes. The shaman's attendants in their green tunics. The guards in their silvery armor.

And at the end, Agdan lies still.

My throat closes.

Time falls away in an instant.

His voice soft and patient like the breeze. His wrinkled hands tracing letters into sand. The scent of wet ink and river clay around us.

"Agdan," I say to the wind, hoping he might somehow hear me and open his eyes.

He might even chide me for being late.

But he remains unmoving.

I kneel beside him, my knees sinking into the wet earth. His hands are thin, spotted with age, still stained with the faint blue of dye. His face is peaceful, but his throat bears a dark wound.

He looks small now. So small.

Lira's hand comes to my shoulder, gentle and comforting.

"He taught you how to read," she says quietly.

"And to write," I answer, tears blurring my sight. "And to think. Above all."

Joru's voice trembles when he speaks. "He was waiting for you, Princess. He said he'd kept something ready for you in his study. A gift, he called it. For your generosity."

I bow my head. "He was generous first. And always."

"I'm glad he keeps the temple's most precious scrolls in his study," Joru adds. "They should still be safe. The raiders didn't get there. I guess the gods were merciful that way."

"I'll see to them later," I manage to answer. "For now, we speak to the prisoner."

Nogas stands a few steps behind me, silent. The rain has washed the blood from his face, but his eyes are darker than before, his gaze heavier.

I glance at him. "Why do you think he only wants to speak with you?"

"Perhaps he wants an outsider, Princess," Nogas says. "Or he believes I am not one of you."

Joru gestures toward the back of the temple. "This way."

We cross the courtyard, past the cracked steps and smoke-stained walls. The prayer banners flutter weakly, edges burnt. Inside, some of the walls bear black and deep red stains. Water drips from the ceiling.

The inner cells of the temple are carved from stone, bare but solid. The prisoner is kept in the smallest one, with a single high window spilling pale light across the floor.

He is bound to a post, wrists chained, mud and blood

caking his skin. His clothes are the same bark and moss disguise as the raiders who ambushed us, though his face is leaner, older. His eyes gleam with something that feels like hunger.

When he sees us, he bares his teeth. "I said I would speak only with the Kalisidlan warrior."

Joru's tone is clipped. "You're speaking to him now."

The raider's eyes move to Nogas. "Then the rest can leave."

Joru nods, then leaves us quietly.

Lira makes a move to follow him, but she takes pause, glancing at me. "Princess?"

I shake my head.

"I stay," I say firmly. "Go. I'll be fine."

She swallows, then nods and follows Joru across the courtyard.

The raider tilts his head. "Princess of Tinigbasan. Your name runs far down the river. Your beauty even farther. The songs do you no justice."

Nogas steps toward him, voice quiet but cold. "If you wish to speak, she stays. The princess is under my protection."

The raider smirks. "I said I would speak only with the warrior of Kalisidlan."

Nogas doesn't move. "She is as good as mine."

Something dangerous glints in the raider's eyes. "Yours?"

Nogas meets his gaze squarely. "She belongs to me, as much as I belong to her."

My stomach tightens. Heat rushes up my neck.

The raider studies him for a long, tense moment. Then

he nods slowly. "Very well. But I have little to say, and it may not please you."

"Then say it."

The man's lips twist into a smile. "Tell me, then, warrior. Why do you think we did not attack Kalisidlan?"

"You fear us," Nogas answers flatly.

"Fear?" The raider laughs, the sound low and wet. "Perhaps. But you should know. Bantawan of Kalisidlan and the Dumalog have made a treaty. We will stand together, against the lords of Hamtic who pretend to own what was never theirs."

A silence coils in the room.

"The attack on your Datu," the raider continues, "was a test. Meant to end him. But you were there. Perhaps Bantawan meant for you to save him, to make Oyong think Kalisidlan still loyal."

Nogas' expression doesn't change, but I feel the tension rippling from him.

"And this time?" I ask.

The raider turns to me, eyes burning. "This time, Princess, it was to prove a point. I was in Kalisidlan. I saw how he fought. We didn't expect your temple guards to have such teeth."

"We made short work of your people," I say, the words cutting as glass. "They'll need more training before they try again."

He laughs delightedly. "Princess, it was never your *life* we wanted. It was you. You were to be taken alive to prove a point. Your life is the prize. You are their jewel, their treasure—but are they ready to go to war for you? We underestimated many things today. But it doesn't matter now."

He leans forward, chains clinking. His gaze slides back to Nogas. "You. You truly are Bantawan's greatest creation. And his greatest threat to all of Hamtic."

Nogas stiffens.

The raider's grin widens. "Perhaps Bantawan wanted you close to her. So when the time comes, you'll already be in her bed. Maybe you already are."

My breath stops.

Before I can move, the raider throws his head back and laughs, wildly, raggedly.

Then he bites hard into the inside of his cheek.

"Stop him!" I shout.

Nogas lunges forward, but it's too late.

The man convulses. Blood spills from his mouth, dark and bubbling. His eyes roll white. He seizes once, twice, then goes still.

The smell of iron fills the room.

Something small and dark falls from his lips and rolls across the floor.

It's a black plum seed, coated with blood.

I drop to my knees beside him, but his chest no longer moves. The veins on his neck have turned black.

"By the gods!" I cry, voice breaking. "Joru!"

The captain bursts in breaths later, sword half-drawn.

"He's dead," I whisper. "He killed himself."

Nogas crouches beside the corpse, the seed between his fingers.

"He said *Bantawan,*" he says in a low voice, so soft I can barely hear him.

"Yes," I breathe, still shaking. "He said your chieftain's name."

Nogas closes his hand around the seed.

The silence that follows feels like the current before a storm.

Outside, the rain falls harder, beating against the temple's stone walls.

CHAPTER 14

Nogas

T HE RAIN FELL AS A WHISPER.

But now it breaks open like a scream.

My entire body tightens, then loosens. The black plum seed falls from my hand and rolls across the stone floor. I rise, but I don't feel myself moving.

I just feel…empty.

Lost.

I don't look at Anini.

I can't.

Before I realize it, I am walking out of the cell, striding through the water-stained halls.

By the time I leave the temple steps, the downpour comes in heavy sheets. It pounds against the ground, washing away the blood, the ash, the dead man's words.

But it can't wash away the words in my head.

Bantawan's greatest creation.

The raider's laughter echoes like thunder behind my skull.

I keep walking. I don't know where. Maybe nowhere. Maybe anywhere that isn't full of ghosts.

"Nogas!"

Her voice cuts through the rain like a blade.

I don't stop.

I hear her feet slapping against stone, lighter and faster than my own.

"Nogas, wait!"

Still, I don't.

I can't.

If I stop, she'll see the storm breaking inside me.

She keeps calling my name, the sound fraying with fury and something else. Fear, maybe.

"Nogas! You will not walk away from me! Not *now!*"

I grit my teeth, jaw locking. "Go back inside, Princess."

"Do not order me!"

The rain stings my face. My sandals sink in mud as I cross the courtyard, past the half-burned pillars and shattered jars. She follows, skirts heavy, soaked to her knees, hair plastered to her face.

"Tell me what he meant," she cries. "Tell me why he said Bantawan's name! Why he said *you*—"

"I don't know!" I shout back, my voice drowned by the downpour.

She keeps coming, stubborn and relentless. "You do! You know something you're not saying!"

"I said I don't!"

"Then why won't you look at me?"

That stops me. Only for a heartbeat.

The wind whips around us. The rain hits hard, then harder, until it feels like knives on my flesh.

"I *am* looking at you," I rasp. "That's the problem."

She freezes, just long enough for her breath to catch. Then she comes at me again, closing the space between us. "Don't you dare twist this! Don't make this about anything else!"

Lightning splits the sky. I see her clearly now. Rain streams down her face, her eyes blazing right through it.

"I watched that man die, Nogas. I watched him choke on his own blood. He said *your name*. He said *Bantawan's name*. What am I supposed to think?"

"Think whatever you want."

She steps closer, chest rising and falling fast. "No. You don't get to say that. You promised me truth."

I clench my jaw and turn away. "Not all truth brings peace, Princess."

"Then let it bring war," she says fiercely. "I am done with falsehoods."

The words hit like a blow.

I walk faster, rain slashing between us, feet splashing through puddles in the muddy grounds leading to the river. She keeps up, almost running now. Her breath comes ragged, furious, and when she catches me again, she grabs my arm with both hands and *pulls.*

"Stop running from me!"

I stop. The sound of our breaths fills the grounds.

"Look at me, Nogas!" Her fingers dig into my arm. "Tell

me what you know. About the raiders. About Bantawan. About *you.*"

"I don't know," I say. "I swear it."

"Then *why* does it sound like a lie?"

"Because it feels like one."

She stares at me, trembling, lips parted, rain sliding down her throat. "You're hiding something."

"I'm hiding *nothing.*"

"Then why are you shaking?" she demands. "Why are you—"

"Because I don't understand any of this!" I snap, stepping closer, closing the space between us. "Because the only thing that makes sense anymore is *you.*"

Her breath catches.

"The only truth I know," I say, the words tearing out of me, "is what I feel for you."

Her tears spill over. They're almost impossible to tell from the rain, but I feel them like my own breath.

"And what do you feel?" she asks, voice cracking. "Tell me. What do you feel for me? Pity? Regret? Guilt?"

I take another step, until I can feel her trembling against me. "No."

"Then *what?*" she cries, fists slamming into my chest, over and over. "Tell me what, damn you!"

I catch her wrists, hard enough that my skin burns at the touch.

"I will destroy every lie they have built around you, Anini. Every chain they try to bind you with. I will burn it all. That is what I feel."

Her breath shudders. "You can't."

"I already have."

Her mouth opens to protest.

But I don't let her.

I crush her against me and kiss her.

It's not gentle.

It's not pure.

It's *everything.*

Rain between our lips. Mud under our feet. Her hands clutching my shoulders.

My grip on her waist tightens, pulling her closer until there's nothing left between us but breath and need and the shiver of what we shouldn't want but can't stop needing.

She gasps against my mouth, and I chase it. All of it. Her sound, her taste, the heat of her pulse.

My hand finds her jaw, thumb tracing the edge of her lips before I kiss her again, deeper this time, until the world goes quiet.

Her fingers slide up into my hair, tangling hard, tugging me down again, rougher and hungrier. The kiss turns savage. Her teeth grazes my lower lip, mine catches hers right back.

The storm doesn't matter. The gods don't matter.

Nothing else matters.

Only this.

Only her.

We break apart only long enough to breathe.

She's crying again, quietly now. But she doesn't step away.

"This changes nothing," she says softly, her voice shaking.

"It changes *everything,*" I murmur, still breathless.

She stares at me, eyes fierce and shining. "Then you'd better be ready for what comes next."

"I already am."

Then I lower my mouth to hers and kiss her again.

Thunder rolls above us. Lightning flares across the sky, and for a heartbeat, she's made of fire and rain and everything I will never deserve.

And I know.

Whatever comes next, I will face them all for her.

I will burn the world until there is nothing left of the lies and her pain.

Because this is the only truth left in me.

CHAPTER 15

Anini

T HE RAIN DROWNS THE WORLD.

The kiss burns through it.

His mouth tastes like storm and fire.

Wild and unyielding. Alive and scorching.

My fingers twist into his soaked hair as if I can hold the moment still. For a heartbeat, I almost believe I can.

But then I pull away, breathless and trembling.

Terrified.

"Y–you'd better be telling me the truth," I say, voice shaking between anger and ache.

His eyes don't leave mine. "I am."

"Swear it."

He reaches behind him, pulls out two daggers from his belt, and places them in my hands. The steel feels cold, heavy, so unlike their perfect lightness when I wielded them against the raiders. The rain runs down the blades like tears.

"Then kill me, Princess," he says softly. "If you doubt me. You have every right to. I swear this to you."

I shake my head, heart thundering. "Don't say that…"

He steps closer, voice steady. "There will be no war. No retribution. You need only tell them there was another raider who got the better of me. That I was killed protecting you."

"Stop—"

"There will be honor in that, Princess. An honor to have served you. An honor to have died in your name. After all this."

I can barely see through the rain. My hands tremble so hard the blades begin to slip from my fingers.

"Don't you dare say that again," I choke out.

He doesn't flinch. "Then prove me wrong. Either way, what I said in the temple was the truth. I belong to you."

Something inside me snaps.

The daggers hit the mud. I lunge at him, his name breaking from my throat like a sob, and then I'm kissing him.

Harder this time. Fiercer. All hunger and lightning and fury.

He catches me by the waist, and I feel his breath shudder against my lips as he pulls me in. I can taste the desperation on him, the promise, the surrender.

My hands slide up his neck, down his shoulders, gripping the cords of muscle slick with rain. He's warm under the cold, impossibly so, and when I press closer, I feel him take a shuddering breath in, as if the air between us has turned to fire.

The world sways around us. I rise on my toes, dragging him down to me, but he wraps his arms around my waist and pulls me up instead.

My feet leave the rain-drenched earth, body flush against his, our soaked clothes plastered together.

It's madness.

It's wrong.

It's everything.

When we finally break apart, both gasping, he presses his lips to my forehead and lowers me back to the ground, but he doesn't let go.

If anything, he pulls me tighter against him.

"Tell me what to do, Princess," he says hoarsely. "Tell me your will. Your choice. And it will be done."

I draw back slightly to look up at him, my heart breaking in every direction.

I can't speak. I can't breathe.

So I whisper the only thing that comes to me.

"Kiss me again."

This time it's slow. Gentle.

The kind of kiss that trembles instead of burns.

He cups my face with both hands, his thumbs brushing away rain or tears. Perhaps both. I can't tell which anymore. Our mouths find each other, not in hunger this time, but in the quiet promise of something that should never exist.

When we part, I lean my forehead against his chest. His heartbeat pounds against my ear. He wraps his arms around me again and I let him. For once, I let someone hold me.

The rain softens. The clouds thin. The faintest gold creeps into the sky.

"It will be sunset soon," I say softly.

"Yes," he murmurs, pulling my cloak tighter around me.

"We should return to the temple."

He nods as he smooths down my hair, then slowly lets me go. He picks up his blades and sheathes them in his belt without a word.

We walk in silence, our shadows long on the wet ground. I walk ahead, my heart still unsteady, but when I turn he's right behind me, silent as a vow.

Before we reach the courtyard, something inside me gives way again.

I turn back. I run to him.

And he catches me.

He barely has time to breathe before I kiss him again. It's quick, reckless, and desperate.

For a moment, everything else fades, leaving only the lingering taste of rain and the heady rush of air between us.

His hand finds the back of my head, his fingers running through my hair, deepening the kiss for a heartbeat before pulling away.

"If you doubt me, kill me, Princess," he rasps, chest heaving. "My life is yours. It will only belong to you until I breathe my last. This is my vow."

I swallow hard, eyes stinging as I trace the strong line of his jaw. "I know."

When we step back into the temple, the guards and handmaidens are all waiting in the hall. Lira and Joru both look up from their conversation, startled.

I see the question in their eyes. I know they see the wet clothes. The silence between us.

But I give them nothing.

Instead, I look at Joru and say, "Captain, the prisoner…"

He nods solemnly. "Dead, Princess. Nothing could be done."

I hear gasps and intakes of breath around me, but I continue. "See to it that his body is burned with the others of his tribe. He took his own life with a poisoned plum."

The captain clears his throat, then nods. "Yes, Princess." He gestures to a few of the temple men, who then bow to me and leave quickly in the direction of the prisoner's cell.

"We will discuss the Dumalog after the sunset rites for Agdan and the scholars," I say, my voice calm. Too calm. "Are we ready?"

Lira clears her throat, then speaks a little hesitantly. "Princess, there is word from Tinigbasan."

A young man steps forward from the cluster of Tinigbasan and temple guards, bowing low. He is soaked to the bone, dressed in the distinct garb of my father's messengers.

"Forgive me, Princess," he says apologetically. "I would not have interrupted your retreat, but I bring a message from the Datu. Please accept my deepest regrets for what happened to the temple and the loss of the shaman, but I have been told to give this to you at the earliest."

He hands me a sealed letter, its edges damp from the rain. I break the wax and read.

My pulse slows with every word.

Datu Radul and Prince Sidlaw of Dalidnon are on their way to Tinigbasan. You are summoned home. Immediately.

I lower the parchment.

The rain starts again, soft yet relentless, seemingly unending.

And Nogas stands behind me, silent as thunder before it strikes.

CHAPTER 16

Shadow of the Trees

Nogas

THE AIR INSIDE THE TEMPLE CURDLES.

The messenger's voice fades like smoke.

And all I can hear is the sound of her breath. It trembles through her, ragged and uneven.

Anini's fingers crush the scroll, her knuckles white. I move next to her, rain still dripping from my cloak, and take it gently from her hands.

She doesn't resist. She just…stares at nothing.

"Lady Lira," I say evenly. "Captain Joru."

Both look at me, stunned and uncertain.

I continue without hesitation. "If you will both pardon me. I will take the princess to her chambers now."

Anini turns to protest, lips parting, but I look to the messenger instead. "The princess thanks you. She will journey home at sunrise. She has travelled a long way.

Tonight, she will attend the funeral rites and rest. Tomorrow, she will speak to Captain Joru and the Temple Guard before we depart."

The man bows, startled by my tone, and backs away. The guards and attendants begin to scatter, unsure what to do with the tension thick in the air.

Without another word, I lift Anini into my arms. She gasps softly, but doesn't fight it. Her pulse flutters against my neck like a trapped bird.

"Where," I ask Lira, "are her chambers?"

The older woman blinks, startled, mouth parting and closing in turn before the words come. "Th-this way."

Lira's sandals slap against the wet stone as she leads us down the hall. The torchlight flickers across the damp walls, painting everything in amber and shadow. I can feel Anini's heartbeat through the wet silk of her robe.

Behind us, Joru begins to give instructions to the remaining guards and scholars to prepare for the rites. I hear thunder groaning above us, but I ignore it.

Halfway down the corridor, Lira finally finds her voice.

"What was in the scroll?" she asks softly.

"Dalidnon," I answer. "The Princess is to return home. She is to wed their prince."

Anini stiffens in my arms. "How…how do you know that?"

I don't answer.

Her voice rises. "Nogas, you didn't even read it. How…"

But the question trails off.

I say nothing. My silence echoes through the hall.

Lira looks from her to me, eyes wide. "Is this true, Princess?"

"Yes." Anini's voice is thin and quiet. "It's true."

We reach the chamber. It's warm inside. The lamps burn low, soft light falling over mats laid thick. The faint scent of jasmine and river reeds waft around us, almost soothingly. Her belongings had already been prepared on the low tables, with scrolls, silks, and small chests of jewelry set out in neat rows.

I lower Anini onto the mats. She doesn't move. Her breath feels tight, pained.

I bow, not meeting her eyes. "Forgive me, Princess. I shall return soon."

Her voice is small. "Where are you going?"

"To check the perimeter. With this rain, the raiders' tracks will vanish quickly. I need to see how they came so close to the temple and the caravan."

She doesn't stop me. She doesn't say *stay*.

So I go.

The forest greets me with silence.

The rain swallows the path behind me, blurring everything into shadow and water. I strip off my heavy cloak, letting it fall to the mud. My spear clatters against a tree. I breathe once. Twice.

Then I *lose it*.

All of it.

I roar. And the sound splits the storm.

Fists slam into bark until blood mixes with rain. My lungs burn. My vision blurs. I hit again and again and again until the world becomes nothing but the rhythm of bone against wood and the raw, useless ache of wanting something I can never have.

My name in her voice.

Her breath against my mouth.

The promise I cannot keep.

"DAMN IT!"

I drive my fist into the trunk one last time, bark splintering, pain flashing white-hot through my arm. I fall to my knees, breath coming in ragged gasps. The storm roars louder, as if the heavens themselves are mocking me.

And then…

A laugh.

Low and deep. So heavy it makes the ground tremble.

I rise slowly, muscles tense, water running down my face.

"Are you planning to make another river?" a voice rumbles. "Perhaps you should think twice. Too much work for a little man."

From the shadows between the trees, something moves.

"I should know," continues the voice. "I made the first one. It wasn't an easy task, but truly worth it in the end."

At first, I think it's the darkness itself. Then it moves closer, and I realize the shadow has a face. A massive shape, with drenched skin the color of spring stones.

He's easily twice my height. Broader than any man I have ever seen. Hands big enough to crush a boulder. His hair is thick and black as midnight, tied back at the nape of his neck. His eyes glint like light cutting through thick clouds.

And yet, he is grinning.

The giant looks…amused.

"Who are you," I say warily, "to disturb my solitude?"

"Solitude?" He chuckles. The sound ripples through the forest. "You call this solitude? I call this a tantrum."

"I have nothing to give you, great one," I say quietly. "I have already given everything that matters."

"Ah," he says, scratching his chin. "A poet. Dangerous creatures, poets. Always bleeding where they shouldn't."

I narrow my eyes. "Name yourself."

He smirks. "Suba."

The name rolls through the air like thunder.

"I am here for my friend Agdan," he adds, stepping toward me with a broad grin. The ground shakes with his weight. "Old man. Small voice. Big heart. Have you met him?"

"I saw his body today," I reply. "But the Princess of Tinigbasan knew him very well."

"Yes," Suba says, tilting his head. "She must have mourned the loss of him. Cried."

"The princess mourns, but she does not cry so much, great one. She is a princess, after all."

"Shame. But quite admirable." He grins wider. "Crying cleanses the soul. You might need that soon, little man."

"I am not in need of cleansing."

"Oh?" He bends down until his face is level with mine. "Then why do you smell of guilt?"

The rain hisses between us.

"I smell of war," I answer flatly.

Suba's grin fades, replaced by something like curiosity.

"You're not lying," he murmurs. "Interesting. Very interesting."

He straightens, looming tall again. "You're caught between too many currents, boy. The blood of the mountain burns in you, but your heart belongs to the river. And if you're not careful, both will drown you."

"I have already drowned," I say.

"Ha!" He laughs, throwing his head back. "Then maybe you'll survive. The drowned are harder to kill."

He starts to turn, fading back into the shadows, but pauses. "Oh, and Nogas?"

I stiffen. "How do you know my name?"

"I know many things." His smile gleams brightly. "Tell your princess her fate is not what her father thinks it is. Tell her…"

He looks toward the horizon, where a faint red glow burns through the clouds.

"Tell her water remembers everything it touches."

Then he's gone.

Just gone.

The forest falls silent again, as if he had never been there.

I stand still for a long time, the rain cooling my skin, blood dripping from my knuckles.

The words echo in my skull.

Water remembers everything it touches.

I look down at my hands, red washing away into the mud.

And I know.

Whatever comes next, I won't survive it unchanged.

CHAPTER 17

Song of the Land

Anini

Rain and ash still cling to the walls, their smells swirling around me.

My father's message lies on the table, but I can feel its weight on my chest like a buried dagger.

Lira sits across from me, wringing her hands. I know she's dying to speak.

"Say it," I murmur.

Her lips press into a thin line. "What did the Datu's message really say? The seafaring kingdom is…?" Her voice trails off.

I nod. "They're sailing for Tinigbasan. Datu Radul and his son, Prince Sidlaw. I am to come home immediately."

Her brows rise. "Prince Sidlaw. He's the one who—"

"Yes." I don't let her finish. "He was…quite bold."

She snorts softly. "You mean insufferable."

That earns a faint smile from me, but it fades quickly.

She leans forward. "But how did Nogas know? He said 'Dalidnon' before you even spoke a word."

I shrug, feigning calm. "He must have overheard the guards at my father's palace. Dalidnon's ships don't move quietly, and neither do their tongues. Court gossip travels faster than lightning."

Lira nods, but her brow still furrows in thought. "True enough. Still…it was quick thinking of him. Removing you from the hall before anyone else could pry. The way he took command—"

"—was quite decisive," I finish.

She smirks. "And effective."

I meet her gaze sharply, but she doesn't look away. "He's done well for himself, that one. Keeps his head, even when everyone else loses theirs."

"Lira," I say carefully, "you're beginning to sound like the maidens at court."

She laughs softly, though her eyes stay on me. "And you, Princess, sound like someone trying very hard not to."

"Not to what?"

"Not to think about him."

I don't comment. Instead, I slowly get to my feet. "Help me change. We have Agdan's rites to attend."

Lira helps me out of my wet robes stained with blood and mud. The fabric clings stubbornly to my skin. She unlaces the back carefully, her fingers brushing the faint bruise along my shoulder.

"He fights well," Lira says after a moment. "So do you." Her eyes meet mine in the bronze mirror. "I don't even know what I will say to Mion when I tell him about this. I don't even know if I should praise him—or slap him senseless for creating a fearsome warrior out of my charge."

I giggle, but it sounds faint, distant.

When I'm finally wrapped in fresh silks of deep river blue, Lira gathers my hair, still damp, and begins to braid it. The rhythmic motion steadies me, though her silence does not.

"Say it, Lira," I tell her. "Whatever you're holding back. This doesn't seem like you at all."

Her reflection watches mine. "You fought bravely, Princess. I feared for you, but more than that, I was proud. You've become something fierce."

I smile faintly. "Not without you and Mion."

"But with *him*?"

"With Nogas?" I turn, meeting her eyes directly.

Her brow arches. "You say his name so easily now."

"Would you rather I stumble over it?"

She shakes her head. "No. But it means something, when a name no longer feels strange."

I look down, fingers tracing the embroidery on my robe. "It's only a name."

"Names carry hearts, Princess." Lira ties off the braid and lays it over my shoulder. "The mountain warrior looks at you like the moon."

I laugh softly. "And the moon can only be looked at, not touched."

"Perhaps," she says, her tone quiet, suspiciously gentle. "But sometimes the moon pulls the tides without meaning to."

Before I can answer, a knock sounds at the door.

Then I hear Joru's voice. "Princess? The rites are prepared. The river awaits."

I stand. "And my shield?"

Joru bows as Lira opens the door. "He waits outside, Princess. He's just returned from his patrol. The perimeter is secure. No signs of spies for now. All tracks lead away from the temple."

"Good," I say, though the relief doesn't reach my voice.

We follow Joru through the long corridors of the temple. The air still carries the faint iron tang of blood, remnants of the morning's attack. The torchlight wavers across old stone carvings, scenes of gods and tides and storms older than the kingdoms themselves.

When we reach the outer steps, the day has deepened into velvety dusk. The rain has slowed to a mist. The river below glows faintly, dark and shimmering like liquid obsidian.

Nogas stands by the lower path, waiting. He's changed into dry clothes. He's wearing a simple brown tunic stitched with the gold of a royal shield, with light armor above it. A new cloak in Tinigbasan colors rests over his shoulders, clasped with my sigil. His hair is damp and loose. In the fading daylight, he looks both fierce and impossibly calm.

He bows as I approach. "Princess. The perimeter is clear. No further movement from the raiders. The forest holds its silence again."

"Good," I say softly. "You may stand beside me during the rites."

"As you wish."

His gaze lingers just long enough to make my pulse stumble. I look away first.

Joru gestures toward the riverbank. "Princess…we have guests."

"Guests?"

He hesitates. "The Lady Kala of the Pearl Waters and her consort, Lord Suba. They came for Agdan's rites. When they heard you were here, they asked to pay respects."

"Who are they?"

"Guardians," Joru says simply. "Of the forest and the deep."

The river comes to life. A ripple moves across its surface, gleaming silver under the torches, followed by another.

Then a soft hum fills the air, a song carried through water.

Shapes begin to move beneath the surface. Many shapes. And then they rise.

One by one, mermaids break the water's skin, their scales flashing like living jewels. Their fins shimmer in layered colors, blues and greens and pale golds that catch every breath of light. Their hair streams behind them like seaweed made of silk.

Their music carries across the riverbank, low and haunting, older than the tongues of men.

Behind them, along the opposite bank, massive figures emerge from the trees. Giants, gray-skinned and broad as the mountains, moving in steady gait. They carry torches the size of masts and bows and clubs carved from whole trees.

The sight stops everyone.

Two figures lead the procession.

A woman glides forward from the river's center. She's

beautiful in a way that hurts to look at. Her hair is blue-black, mimicking the surface of the sea before dawn. Her pale skin glows faintly, and her eyes shimmer like molten pearl.

When she reaches the shallows, the gray-skinned giant beside her, towering and muscular, with his long black hair tied back, extends a hand. The water around them swirls softly, as if alive.

She takes his hand, and as she steps onto the bank, her tail begins to dissolve into legs. Silk ripples from her waist down, forming a gown so dark and fluid it looks like midnight water caught mid-wave.

Joru bows low. "My lady. My lord."

"Captain Joru." The woman smiles, her voice like the echo of waves in a cave.

The giant's grin is broad and warm like firelight. "You have my thanks, Captain. I would have preferred not to visit under such grim tidings, but Agdan was a dear friend."

The mermaid's gaze finds me. "And you must be the Princess of Tinigbasan. The jewel of the river kingdom. I am Kala of the Pearl Waters. This is my consort, Suba of the Hamtic Peaks."

I bow. "Anini, daughter of Oyong. Welcome to our shores, Lady Kala, Lord Suba. You bring great honor to Shaman Agdan's rites with your presence."

Kala's eyes soften. "You speak like your mother."

My heart skips. "You knew her?"

"I did. Rumina was dear to me." Kala steps closer, her dress whispering like surf. "I found her adrift at sea long ago, before she ever became Dayang. It was the scholars of this very temple who raised her. When Oyong came for her hand, she went to the Tinigbasan court, but her heart always belonged to the waters."

My throat tightens. "I never knew that."

"She would be proud of you, Anini." Kala touches my cheek lightly, cool as the tide. "May the world remember you as the river remembers the rain. For all eternity."

Suba rumbles a laugh. "You have her eyes, little one. But not her softness. I see steel that burns."

Kala swats him lightly. "Ignore him. He means to praise you, though his tongue still trips over poetry."

The giant grins down at me, then gestures to Nogas, who stands just behind me, silent and unmoving. "So this is the princess' shield?"

I nod. "He is my protector. Nogas of Kalisidlan."

Suba laughs low. "I didn't recognize him at first, standing so still. The last time I saw him, he was busy trying to knock down my trees with his fists."

I whirl around to look at Nogas. "You met him?"

"Oh yes," the giant answers. "A furious little current of a man. I thought he'd carve a new river before the night was done."

Nogas' voice is steady. "You should have stopped me, great one."

"I rather enjoyed the show, truth be told."

Kala sighs. "Men." She reaches for my hand, then gestures toward the water. "Come, Princess. Let us honor Agdan and the temple folk. The river awaits."

Joru bows deeply. "As you wish, my lady."

The procession moves to the riverbank, where pyres of woven reeds float on the water, each bearing flowers, scrolls, and the carved wave symbols of the fallen. The mermaids begin to sing again, their voices rising and falling like the tide. The giants raise their torches high, their flames reflected in the water like a thousand trembling stars.

Kala steps into the river. Her voice, deep and melodic, joins the song, a current that seems to pull at the heart itself.

I bow my head. The music moves through me, and I feel it—the pull of the river, the pulse of the sea, the breath of the sunset sky.

Beside me, Nogas stands still as stone, eyes on the flames.

And when the pyres begin to drift downstream, disappearing one by one into the glowing dark, I swear the water itself whispers.

I remember every stone I touch.

I remember everything.

CHAPTER 18

Challenge of the Veil

Nogas

THE RIVER BURNS LIKE A TRAIL OF STARS.

The flames of the funeral pyres drift downstream, turning to embers in the current, then swallowed by the dark. The mermaids' voices fade into low hums.

Beside me, Anini stands motionless, her face carved by torchlight.

Lady Kala steps toward the bank, her dress flowing like water turned to silk.

"The rites are done," she says softly, voice rippling through the hush. "But the river still remembers. Princess of Tinigbasan, before you leave these waters, I would speak with you. Come with me to the place where the fire meets the stone, a cradle where the sun hides, yet still burns in the dark."

Anini bows her head. "I will go."

Lord Suba snorts, inclining his head toward me. "Then the little man needs to come too. The princess will need a guard in the dark. Not all currents are kind."

Kala narrows her eyes. "You cannot bring mortals there, Suba. You know the law. The veil cannot hold their breath."

He smiles down at her, unbothered. "Let the princess bring her shadow, my love. He bites, but he follows well."

Kala's voice hardens, like ice under current. "No. He cannot cross. He is not of the blood."

I bow slightly. "My duty is to guard the path the princess walks, great lady. I must go where she treads."

Anini turns to Kala. "Wait. Can he not come at all?"

The mermaid's eyes glimmer with something ancient. "No mortal walks where the boon rests. Only those of the old blood are welcome. They are the sea's chosen, the blessed of the river, and the kin of the first flame. You are tied to me through your mother's boon. He is not."

Anini hesitates, then says quietly, "Can you not make an exception?"

Kala shakes her head. "This is no court, child. There are no exceptions in the old laws."

"Then perhaps I can ask for one, great lady," Anini says softly, steadily, but the words cut through the air. "Nogas belongs to me, just as I belong to him."

The sound shatters the night.

Those of the temple and Anini's court all freeze. Joru stares at the princess with wide eyes, while Lira's breath catches loudly, her hand flying to her mouth.

The mermaids gasp, tails flicking the surface into silver ripples. The giants murmur, their deep voices vibrating through the ground. Even the river seems to recoil, as if the earth itself is listening.

Kala stares at Anini in disbelief. Suba blinks once, then bursts into deep, thunderous laughter.

I can't move. My pulse hammers so hard it hurts.

Those words.

The same words I spoke to the Dumalog prisoner not a day ago. And now *she* says them.

Calmly. Proudly. As if she means it.

Kala's voice, when it returns, is a low tide of warning. "You speak boldly, Princess. Dangerous words, even for one with river blood."

"Then let them be dangerous," Anini replies, chin high. "Danger is something I have learned to embrace."

Suba leans closer to Kala. "Let the boy come, sea-wife. If she claims him, the bond is sealed already. The river will not reject what's been declared."

Kala gives him a sharp look. "Enough. The girl may cross under her mother's boon, but the mountain warrior cannot. His heart is stone, his blood too mortal. He would die before the veil even touched him."

Suba tilts his head toward me. "Then perhaps he should *earn* his place."

I meet his gaze. "Name your price, great one."

He chuckles. "Fight me, little man. If you survive, the river will know your blood. If you win—" he bares his teeth in a grin "—I owe you a boon."

Kala's voice lashes out like a whip. "Suba!"

But the words are already leaving my mouth. "I accept. I challenge you to the Rite of Binding Blood."

Everything stops.

The giants erupt into murmurs once more. The mermaids dive and resurface, singing fragments of strange songs in alarm.

Even Kala's eyes flare with something like fear. Or fury, perhaps.

"Do you understand what you invoke, mortal?" she hisses. "That rite was forged when gods still walked this earth. Blood against blood. Honor for honor. Strength for strength."

"I do," I say. "And I will not yield."

Suba laughs, booming and delighted. "Ha! Brave fool. I've not fought a mortal under moonlight in an age."

Anini's voice cuts through his laughter. "Stop this!"

I turn to her. "Princess—"

"Don't," she warns. "You'll be crushed."

I bow my head. "If I am, then let it be for you."

"Don't make this sound noble." Her voice trembles with anger, or something close to it. "You're doing this for pride."

I look at her. At the fire in her eyes, at the river light caught in her hair.

"No, Princess. For *belonging.*"

Her breath shakes, shoulders heaving.

Lira moves closer to Anini, face pale as she clutches the princess' arm. "This is madness! Princess, make him stop!"

Anini's eyes never leave mine. "I cannot. The challenge is spoken. You heard my shield. The river hears it."

Lira turns to me. "Think twice, mountain-born. Look at him! He could snap you in half!"

I smile faintly. "Lady Lira…when a stone breaks into

smaller pieces, does it make it any less of a stone? There are more of them then. Faster. Perhaps sharper."

She stares at me, speechless.

I turn to Anini, bending down to lay my belt, daggers, and spear at her feet. I strip off my armor, the clasps clinking softly, then my tunic. The river wind stings against my skin.

"When you said you would die for me," she tells me softly, "I didn't expect it to be so soon."

I kneel before her, head bowed. "By your leave, Princess."

Her voice trembles. "Granted."

When I stand, the world has narrowed to moonlight and shadow.

The river glows faintly, its surface rippling. Suba, now bare to the waist like me, wades into it, the current swirling around his knees. His skin gleams like wet rock, muscles coiled with ancient power. Around him, the mermaids form a circle, their tails cutting the water into glittering arcs.

The giants chant, low and rhythmic, stamping the earth in time with the flow of the river. The scholars, guards, and maidens all stand back, their faces pale. Even Joru looks uneasy, his hand on his blade but too afraid to draw it.

Kala steps to the bank once more, her expression grave. "The rite is bound by witness. When blood meets blood, the fight begins. No retreat. Only death or surrender, whichever comes before. The currents decide."

"Perfect," Suba says, spreading his arms. "Show me what the mountain taught you, little spark."

I step into the river. The current tugs at me, strong and relentless.

I have fought my whole life. What's another fight?

And so my pulse steadies.
Across from me, Suba grins, teeth gleaming like moons.
Kala raises her hand.
"Begin."
The instant her palm drops, Suba moves.
I take a breath, then run toward him.
And, in a giant spray of silver, the river around us erupts.

CHAPTER 19

Binding of Blood

Anini

THE TORCHES AROUND THE RIVERBANK CRACKLE AND hiss, their light flickering over the black water.

The air smells of wet stone and smoke. The mermaids' songs have faded to a tense hum. The giants are silent now, their heavy breaths rumbling like distant thunder.

The moon hangs low and full, its reflection trembling across the current, bright and broken yet somehow alive.

And between those two reflections, Nogas and Suba face each other.

Suba stands knee-deep in the river, his gray skin glinting under the moonlight, muscles shifting like slabs of rock. His hair is bound high, the ends dripping with water, his eyes bright and wild.

Nogas faces him with nothing but the currents at his waist. No armor, no weapons. Only his body, lean and taut, shoulders squared, breathing steady. He's already soaked, but he looks utterly still.

The air between them is tight enough to snap.

Kala lowers her hand.

"Begin."

Suba moves first.

The river explodes.

He charges forward, the water erupting around his legs, and swings a fist the size of a boulder toward Nogas' head. Nogas ducks, the punch whistling past him and slamming into the surface, sending a spray like rain across the bank.

The impact alone would have crushed bone.

Nogas pivots and slams his elbow into Suba's ribs. The sound it makes is dull, solid. He ducks again, dodging another swing, water splashing over his face.

I hold my breath, clutching the edge of my cloak.

Suba grins, teeth gleaming. "Too slow, mountain boy!"

Nogas doesn't answer. He steps back, shoulders rolling, breath measured. I can see how he studies Suba's rhythm, how his eyes track every motion.

The rise of Suba's arm, the flex of his knee before he swings.

Nogas is *watching*. Waiting.

Suba lunges again, aiming high. Nogas drops under the blow, the movement so clean it's almost beautiful. He drives a fist into Suba's stomach, not to hurt, but to disrupt balance. When Suba stumbles half a step, Nogas spins behind him, his body moving like water across rock.

The river churns around them. The giants roar their approval.

Suba turns, snarling, throwing an upward strike that tears through the air. Nogas sidesteps, the wind of it brushing his jaw. He counters with a sharp strike to Suba's ribs, then leaps backward, avoiding another hit.

Each movement is perfect. No wasted strikes. No hesitation.

But Suba's strength is relentless. He sweeps an arm through the water, knocking Nogas' legs out from under him. Nogas crashes into the river, disappearing beneath the surface.

Lira gasps. "No!"

Then he rises—*erupts*—from the water, gasping, his hair plastered against his face, and dives forward again. Suba swings down. Nogas twists, catches the giant's arm under his own, and rolls his entire body around it. The momentum drags Suba off-balance, his feet slipping on the stones.

Nogas plants his knee against Suba's back and wrenches the arm upward, using his entire weight to leverage the joint. Suba bellows in pain, jerking violently to free himself, but Nogas doesn't release. He adjusts, then repositions.

Every movement is fluid, almost practiced. And undeniably merciless.

The river boils with their motion.

Nogas slips behind Suba again, water swirling around them, and in a single, seamless motion, locks his arm around the giant's neck.

A choke from the rear. It looks tight. Inescapable.

Suba thrashes, but Nogas holds, his legs hooked around the giant's torso, his arm pressing against the throat.

The world becomes sound and struggle.

Suba's fists crash into the water, sending up geysers that spray across the bank. Each strike would shatter a man's ribs, but Nogas is always one breath ahead. He tightens when Suba loosens, adjusts when he jerks, forcing the giant's body to work against itself.

He's not stronger.

But he is smarter. Faster.

Suba staggers forward, gasping, trying to throw him off. Nogas' face is buried against the giant's shoulder, his body taut, veins straining. His forearms tremble with the effort, but he doesn't let go.

The sound of the current fills everything.

Suba stumbles, legs buckling. Nogas tightens, just once, and…

A resounding crack.

Then another.

And once more.

Suba strikes the ground thrice.

The sound of surrender.

The stones beneath their feet split. The river shudders. Water surges upward between them, bursting like a massive geyser and crashing back in a roar. The impact sends ripples racing to the banks, soaking everyone watching.

It's over.

The roar from the giants splits the night. The mermaids sing again, their voices fierce and high, echoing off the cliffs. Kala's eyes are wide, unblinking. Even Lira is frozen, her hand over her mouth. Next to her, Joru is still as stone, his face pale.

Nogas releases the hold and jumps down to the water,

hunched over, shoulders heaving. His skin gleams like bronze under the moonlight.

The river churns around him restlessly.

It knows something impossible has happened.

Suba stays still for a heartbeat, coughing, the water dripping from his hair. Then he starts to laugh.

A deep, thunderous sound that shakes the world.

He turns, still breathing hard, and extends one enormous hand. Nogas stares at it for a moment, then takes it. Suba's palm could crush his, but instead the giant grips it tight and pulls him upright.

For a moment, they stand there, warrior and mountain. Both soaked, both shaking, both alive.

And then Suba's voice rolls low. "The water will never forget you now, little man."

The giants pound their chests with their fists. The mermaids' song rises, haunting yet somehow joyous.

Nogas lowers his head, voice rough but steady. "Then I will never forget it, great one. Neither will I forget how honorably you fought."

And as the cheers crash over the water, as the moon spills its light across them both, I realize something seemingly irrevocable has changed.

The river didn't just witness him tonight.

It claimed him.

And I will never be able to look at him the same way again.

CHAPTER 20

Flame of the Stone

Nogas

Tʜᴇ ʀɪᴠᴇʀ ʜᴀs sᴇᴛᴛʟᴇᴅ ɪɴᴛᴏ ʀɪᴘᴘʟᴇs, ᴛʜᴇ sᴜʀғᴀᴄᴇ dappled with reflected torches and the ghosts of the stars.

The mermaids rise first, graceful and regal, their tails glinting in the moonlight. At a nod from Lady Kala, they bow low to the princess, their foreheads touching the water. Then, with a single sweep of their fins, they dive beneath the surface and vanish into the deep.

The giants follow.

Each one pounds a fist against his chest, the sound like thunder rolling through the forest. Then they, too, bow to Anini before turning and disappearing into the trees, their silhouettes fading like mountains walking away.

Only we remain. The temple guards, drenched and wide-eyed, stand in front of the handmaidens and scholars, who are still whispering prayers. Lira clutches her shawl to her chest, staring at the river wide-eyed. The smell of wet earth hangs heavy in the night around us.

Captain Joru rushes toward me and Suba with two of his men, each carrying clean cloth for us to dry off with.

"Lord Nogas, please take this," says one of the guards. "You're bleeding."

I take the cloth and nod my thanks. Another guard presses a cup of water into my hand, but I barely feel it. My breath still burns. My arms shake from where I held the choke too long. My body aches from the impact of Suba's strikes and the river's current and rocks.

I ignore them all.

But I turn toward her.

The princess stands a few paces away, still as carved stone, her face unreadable in the light cast by the torches and the moon. The hem of her robe is soaked from the spray.

She looks at me, and in that moment, I wish I could take her in my arms and tell her, *I will never stop fighting for you.*

So I kneel instead. My knees hit the mud, hard.

"Forgive me, Princess," I say quietly. "Had I died, I would not have served you as I swore to. I can only hope that my victory brings you honor."

For a long time, she doesn't move. She doesn't even speak.

Only the wind answers.

Then she takes one slow step forward, and another. Her hand trembles slightly as she bends and picks my cloak up from the ground. The fabric is streaked with grass and earth.

But she shakes it out gently, dusting it off with her own hands, and places it around my shoulders herself.

The murmurs around us fall silent.

Everyone is watching. Even Suba, still panting from the fight, stops grinning for a moment and looks almost… impressed.

Anini's hands linger against my neck for a heartbeat before she pulls away.

"Rise, Shield of Tinigbasan," she says. Her voice is steady, though her throat trembles.

I stand, heart pounding in my ears.

"Put on your tunic and weapons," she continues, straightening. "We leave soon. Lady Kala and Lord Suba will guide us. The return to Tinigbasan begins at dawn."

Something in her tone changes when she says that last word.

Dawn.

It lands heavy between us, a reminder of what awaits her then.

Prince Sidlaw. Datu Radul.

Her father.

The alliance with Dalidnon.

Anini turns to Joru and Lira, her voice brisk now, full of command.

"Double the temple guards. No one rests until the perimeter is secured for the night. Captain Joru, see to the wounded before they retire. Have the guards patrol the archives and Agdan's study. The raiders might come back."

Joru bows. "As you command, Princess. The scrolls and trinkets you brought are already in the shaman's private study. They should be safe there."

Anini nods. "Good. Lira, see that everything is accounted for. I shall review them myself before we hand them over to the scholars. Once the work is done, all will have supper and rest for the journey tomorrow. And, Captain, we shall discuss at dawn how to deal with the Dumalog and how to repair and secure the temple, before I depart for Tinigbasan."

Her words are crisp and disciplined, but I can still see the faint tremor in her fingers.

I pull on my tunic and strap on my belt and daggers. The movement steadies me despite the pain in my limbs. As Anini speaks, I fall easily into the rhythm of command again.

When she finishes, I face the Temple Guard gathered before us.

"Captain," I say, "have two guards patrol the outer ridge until sunrise. Any tracks in the mud, any traces of movement, have them report to me directly once the princess and I return. The Dumalog might use the cover of dark to prepare for another raid at dawn."

Joru nods. "Understood, Shield."

Kala and Suba approach then, moving like shadow and storm.

Suba looks as if he's already forgotten his defeat, his chuckles booming as he slaps me once, hard, on the shoulder. "You fight well, little man. Too well. Remind me never to spar with you when I've eaten."

Kala rolls her eyes. "You nearly drowned him, Suba."

He smiles down at her. "A fair exchange, my love. He nearly strangled me."

The mermaid's smile is faint but weary. "I see why the river will remember him."

She turns to Joru, her expression softening. "Captain, we mourn your loss. Agdan was wise beyond measure. May the next shaman be strong enough to bear the weight of what he left behind."

Joru bows, visibly moved. "You honor us, Great Lady of the Pearl Waters."

Kala looks at Anini. "Princess, we must go. The hour grows late."

She steps into the water, her legs already beginning to shimmer, dissolving into a sleek tail as the river welcomes her back.

Suba dips his head to Anini. "You first, Princess of Steel. The current awaits."

Kala raises her arm, and the river stirs, like a living creature responding to her commands. "This way is faster. Through the eternal veil. You will be home before the night ends."

Lira clutches Anini's sleeve, panic flashing in her eyes. "Princess, please. You don't have to—"

Anini lays a gentle hand over hers. "It's alright, Lira. I shall see you shortly."

Lira's lips tremble. "Then promise me. Be safe." Her gaze cuts toward me. "And *you*. Make sure she is."

I bow, then sling my spear across my back. "I will, Lady Lira."

Anini turns to me, then steps toward the water where Kala waits. Her hand finds mine.

"Come," she says.

"Breathe deeply when the veil pulls," Kala says. "It may feel like drowning, but it passes."

Before I can ask what that means, the water opens around us. For a moment, I feel the pull, cold and crushing, swallowing everything. My lungs seize, my body dragged through dark and depth.

Then I break through.

We emerge gasping into air that smells of salt and mountain wind.

The moon is still above us, but higher now, sharper and clearer. We stand on a narrow plateau surrounded by mist. Below, the ocean spreads out like glass, the waves so far down they look like moving smoke.

Kala holds Anini steady by the hand, her voice calm. "Breathe, Princess. It will get better soon."

Anini leans against me, her breathing shallow and quick, her hair streaming with droplets that glow like starlight.

Suba bursts through next, roaring with laughter, shaking the spray from his arms. "Ha! The veil still bites!"

Kala sighs. "Stop being so dramatic."

He grins broadly and takes her hand.

Then Kala gestures around us. The air hums faintly, the rocks glowing under the moonlight, the wind curling like fire without flame.

"Welcome," she says softly, "to the most sacred place

in all the isles of Hamtic. This is where flame first met stone. Where the land itself was born."

I look down at the sea, then at Anini beside me. She's still catching her breath, her hand tightening around mine.

In that moment, I understand why people kneel before gods.

CHAPTER 21

Gift of Gold

Anini

THE SPRING CRADLES US IN HEAT AND LIGHT.

The water bubbles softly around my arms, steam rising into the cold night air like the breath of the earth itself. The scent of the air is iron, salt, and something faintly sweet, like crushed petals.

My lungs still ache from the crossing, but when I blink, the world comes alive in vivid colors.

We are standing in a pool carved into the side of a mountain, the surface reflecting stars and the sea far below. The moon sits heavy and bright on the horizon, silver spilling over the black water.

Beyond us, the land slopes upward into terraces of pale stone and dark earth. Nestled among them is an enormous structure, seemingly half-grown and half-built, an earthen palace of pillars and domes shaped by time itself. It glows faintly from within.

Kala draws herself out of the spring first. As she steps onto the smooth rock, her tail splits apart, reshaping into long legs. The water threads through her skin as her dark gown blooms over her body. When she turns back to us, she looks nothing less than divine, her eyes reflecting both the sea and the stars.

She raises her hands and the pool parts, pulling me and Nogas gently onto the dry stone. My body feels heavier in the air, my skin still tingling from the warmth of the spring. With a tilt of her head, a soft breeze surrounds us, pulling the water from my clothes and hair.

"This," Kala says, gesturing around us, "is where the water met the stone. But when the two embraced, flame was born. These springs rose from that union, and from them flowed the first river of Hamtic."

My breath catches. "Then the legend is true?"

"Of course it is true," Suba declares. "Not as grand as the storytellers make it sound, but true enough." He stands half-shadowed behind her, enormous and delighted. "Took me many, many sun-cycles to carve my way down from the peaks toward the sea. My lady met me halfway. Our home has been here ever since."

Before Kala can protest, Suba sweeps her off her feet and kisses her, fiercely and hungrily, like the earth claiming the tide. The sound of it echoes.

Kala breaks away with a breathless laugh, punching his chest. "Enough, you great fool. We have guests."

Nogas and I exchange a glance. His mouth quirks faintly. My cheeks burn hot despite the cool night. I look away first.

Kala smooths her hair and turns to me, her smile softening. "Forgive us, Princess. The reason we brought you here is not only to share our supper but to fulfill a promise. To grant you your mother's boon. Let us call it a gift. A token of friendship between her and me."

I swallow, nodding. "I am honored, great lady."

"Come," Kala says simply, and gestures upward.

From the edges of the terraces, shapes emerge. There are men and women with long dark hair, their clothing cut from silk and shadow, their eyes reflecting the moonlight. Their ears taper slightly, finned like delicate coral. Some carry baskets of fruit and flowers, others pitchers of drink. They move with the fluid grace of waves, forming a quiet procession along the path.

The path winds up toward the palace. The structure itself is massive, sculpted to fit Suba's height, its doors tall enough for giants. The columns are carved with spirals of shells and scaled patterns that gleam faintly in the torchlight. The floor beneath us is smooth and warm, veined with glowing metals like molten gold.

Suba bounds ahead, his booming voice filling the air. "Welcome, welcome! My friends, tonight we feast with the daughter of Dayang Rumina! Bring your best wine. No, I mean the *good* kind, the one that tastes like fire!"

Kala rolls her eyes fondly. "He has been waiting hundreds of cycles for guests. A chance to show off."

Suba stops by an enormous vase overflowing with white-and-yellow flowers, each with five waxy petals.

He plucks a handful, their scent spilling into the air, sweet and clean, like morning sun after rain.

He turns and offers them to me with a bow. "I call these *river-meets-the-sun*, Princess. The currents coming together under the grace of light. They only grow here, on this land."

I accept the flowers carefully, their petals warm against my palm. "They are beautiful. Thank you, Lord Suba."

Nogas inclines his head. "Very beautiful indeed, great one."

Kala smiles, eyes bright. "Then let these flowers mark my boon. You may bring one across the veil, Princess. It will never die as long as your mother's blood endures. When you hold it, you may call on me. And I shall come, wherever you may be. This is the bond between us."

I nod, awed. "I will honor it, great lady."

Kala steps close, her hand cool against my cheek. She blesses one of the flowers, murmuring softly, then tucks it behind my ear. "It will live as you do, our beautiful princess." She leans down and presses a kiss to my forehead. "Now, shall we have supper?"

The great hall of the earthen palace glows golden, lit by bowls of flame and crystal that cast ripples of light across the walls. The tables are carved from single slabs of stone, wide enough for a giant's arm span, yet set delicately with cups and dishes that gleam like seashells.

We sit among them, Nogas to my right, Kala and Suba at the head. The men and women pour wine the color of amber and bring platters of roasted meat, wild roots, and fruits that shimmer faintly.

Conversation flows as freely as the wine. Suba talks more than anyone.

"I was the first to climb the mountains of fire," he says, pounding a fist over his heart. "When I reached the highest peak, I looked down and saw her. My lady of the depths! I thought, *what fool carves mountains while beauty swims beneath the world?*"

Kala laughs, covering her face with her hand. "He leaves out how many times he fell from the peaks…trying to look."

He winks. "Only once. Or twice. Maybe ten times. But when I finally reached the shore, she was there, and she had already made the tide to meet me."

The laughter that ripples around the table feels light and human, though I know none of them truly are.

When the laughter fades, Kala looks toward me, her voice softer. "It was not as simple as he claims. There were rituals…old rites that bound the elements. Rites we had to win to prove ourselves to the heavens. But those are not for mortal ears. Some truths beyond the veil are better kept unspoken."

I nod, understanding. "You sound as though you have carried those truths a long time."

Kala's smile is wistful. "Longer than most rivers remember, Princess."

Later, as the meal quiets, Nogas speaks, his voice low. "Lord Suba…you were a friend to Shaman Agdan. Why did you not avenge his death?"

The question hangs, sudden and heavy.

Suba breathes out slowly, the mirth leaving his face. "Because the lives and deaths of mortals are not ours to claim.

We are not guardians of vengeance. We are bound only by what we give. Our boon can only be granted once before it must be renewed. It is not our place to meddle."

Kala nods. "We cross the veil only when the world calls us, not when pride tempts us. Mortals," she adds, her eyes meeting mine, "have long since been reduced by greed. They turn gifts into weapons, and love into conquest. That is why what is beyond the veil must stay beyond it. Some powers are not meant to be held."

Silence follows her words, deep and thoughtful.

Then Suba rises from his seat, his great shadow falling across the table. "But some things, at least, can be shared."

He strides to the far wall and lifts something resting there. In his massive hands is a great golden shield, round and radiant, shaped like the sun itself. Its face gleams with etchings of five rays that seem to pulse faintly in the light.

He brings it to Nogas and sets it before him with both hands. "This was mine once. When I was still a warrior of the peaks, staring across the water at the beauty I thought too far to reach."

Nogas looks up at him. "And now, Lord Suba?"

He grins, baring sharp white teeth. "Now I know nothing is too far. Not when you have the will to fight for it."

Suba glances at me, then at Nogas again. "Keep it, little man. I'm glad my lady convinced me to have it forged smaller as a memento of my life long gone. Let it remind you that even the sun bows to the water in time. This will be the token of my boon. Call for me with it, and your will be done."

I look at Nogas as he stands and reaches out, hands

steady, and lifts the golden shield. The light catches across his face.

For a fleeting moment, I see him not as a warrior or a shadow, but as something brighter, forged by the world itself.

Though the night is peaceful and still, I cannot let go of the feeling that the flame Suba spoke of, the one born of water and stone, has just found a new place to burn.

CHAPTER 22

Nogas

THE NIGHT IS DEEPER NOW.

The dark is thicker that the stars seem close enough to touch. The air hums with heat from the springs. The water glows faintly under the moon, gold running like veins through the stone.

Kala stands at the edge of the pool, the steam curling around her like smoke around fire. Her eyes, pale and endless, flick between me and the princess.

"It is time," she says softly. "Step in, and you will surface near the temple."

Her voice carries that strange resonance, the sound of waves against the bones of the earth.

Suba smiles widely as he stands beside her, arms crossed over his chest. "And you will surface drenched and dizzy, little ones. But alive! I am certain this will not be the last time I see you."

Kala sighs, though her smile betrays affection. "You should learn not to speak over farewells, beloved."

Then, to us, her tone changes, heavier, carrying ancient, unspoken truths.

"Remember this, both of you. Every boon demands a choice. It cannot be ignored. When the time comes, decide with your whole heart, or be consumed by what you leave unchosen."

Her words settle like a weight between my ribs. Anini's breath catches. I glance down at her, and her eyes, dark and glistening under the moon, meet mine.

We both nod.

Suba gives a booming laugh, stepping back. "Go then, river and flame. Go before my lady grows sentimental. I do not wish to see her cry on such a beautiful night."

Kala gestures delicately with her hands, and the water begins to stir. The surface ripples, spinning slowly, then faster, until the center dips inward, forming a whirling pool of gold and black.

"Fare you well, Princess and Shield," she says, before the water begins to rise.

The air tightens. I can feel the pull even before we move.

I shift the shield, Suba's sun, into my left hand. With my right, I reach for Anini's waist, wrapping my free arm around her.

"Hold on, Princess," I murmur.

She tilts her face up to mine. The light dances on her skin, pale and alive.

I can't stop myself.

Before the whirlpool swallows us, before the night disappears, I lean in and kiss her.

Her lips part in shock, and she gasps softly. Then her hands rise, trembling, curling around the back of my neck. She kisses me back, fiercely. The heat of her mouth, the press of her body…it feels as if the world has vanished, and only the sound of her heartbeat remains.

The current surges around us.

And then the world turns upside down.

The pull tears through my chest, water swallowing us whole. For a breath, there is no sound, only the crushing dark and her fingers gripping my hair and tunic.

Then…air.

We burst through the surface, gasping, drenched and blinking rapidly, the river of the temple spreading wide around us. The sky here is softer, the stars dimmed by clouds.

Lira is the first to spot us. She rushes forward from the bank, Joru close behind her, both wrapped in cloaks against the night.

Her eyes widen at the sight of us, our arms still tangled together. She says nothing. Neither does Joru. Instead, he clears his throat.

"The temple is secure, Princess," he reports stiffly. "But perhaps it would be wise to ask your father for reinforcements when you return home."

Anini gathers herself, still breathless. "Of course. I will have Mion select them personally once we are back in Tinigbasan."

Lira approaches quietly, pressing a dry cloak and cloth

into Anini's hands, fussing, wiping strands of hair from her face. She notices the flower tucked behind Anini's ear, glistening like glass.

"A gift from Lady Kala," Anini says softly.

Lira only nods.

I take a fresh cloak from her, bowing slightly. "My thanks, Lady Lira." I wrap it around my shoulders, feeling the warmth bleed into my skin, then stoop to lift the shield once more.

Joru studies it closely, eyes alight. "A fine weapon, Shield. The craft of Suba himself, I'd wager."

I nod once. "He gave it freely. I intend to make it worthy of him."

Anini turns to me. "You should change. I will see you shortly in Shaman Agdan's study."

Joru steps in. "I will escort the Princess and Lady Lira. The Shield should see to his preparations."

Anini nods. "Very well."

As they turn to leave, Lira holds Anini close, wrapping the cloak tightly around her shoulders. The two of them walk together toward the temple steps, the lanterns painting their forms in pale gold.

Before she disappears inside, Lira glances back at me, her eyes questioning and protective.

I give a single nod. She breathes out, her stance relaxing, then she follows Anini through the doors.

Silence returns.

I make a slow circuit around the temple grounds, the new shield in my arm, its surface catching the dim torchlight. No signs of raiders. No fresh tracks. Only the smell of rain and the whisper of leaves.

Still, the restlessness gnaws at me.

When I finally return inside, the corridors are quiet. My chamber is a small room near hers. It's simple and clean, the faint scent of cedar in the woven mats. I set the shield down and realize only then how heavy it was. My arms tremble faintly.

I change quickly. Fresh tunic, dry trousers, belt fastened tight, with the spear slung across my back. The familiar weight steadies me.

I step back into the hall. Through the door of Anini's chamber, I hear the soft murmur of voices, hers and Lira's, and the faint rustle of cloth.

I turn away and make my way to the courtyard. A guard bows and gestures toward heavy wooden doors tucked at the end of the opposite wing.

Inside Agdan's private study, the air feels different.

The walls are carved from pale stone, etched with water symbols. Shelves line the chamber, heavy with scrolls, tablets, and carved wooden artifacts. Mats of fresh reed cover the floor, where new offerings from Tinigbasan have been carefully laid out in neat rows. I see trinkets, coins, and small woven charms nestled among stacks of scrolls. Small oil lamps burn in the corners of the room, the smoke trailing upward like thin, steady columns.

It feels untouched. Ancient, yet alive.

I pace once, twice, unable to keep still. The night presses close around me.

Then the door slides open.

Anini steps in.

Her hair is damp but loosely tied back, a few strands

clinging to her cheeks. She wears a light gold shift beneath her cloak, the fabric soft and gleaming in the lamplight. Her feet make no sound on the stone floor. Our eyes meet, and for a moment, everything in me stops.

I cross the room before I even think.

When I reach her, she opens her mouth to speak, but I don't let her. I catch her by the waist, lift her into my arms, and crush my mouth to hers.

She gasps, her hands finding my shoulders, clutching hard. The kiss deepens, tasting of salt and fire and everything forbidden.

Her body melts against mine, fingers sliding up the back of my neck, tangling in my hair. The world narrows to breath and skin and the wild drum of our hearts.

She pulls back, just enough for air, whispering my name, and then she kisses me, fiercer this time, her mouth open, her breath shaking.

My hand finds the small of her back, drawing her closer still. Her cloak falls away, pooling at our feet.

And for a heartbeat, there is no war.

No treaties. No lies.

No kingdom. No Sidlaw.

Only her heat. Only her breath.

Only the truth that burns between us.

CHAPTER 23

Honor of the Gods

Anini

HIS MOUTH IS STILL ON MINE WHEN WE CRASH INTO the edge of the table.

Scrolls tumble, a few ceramic jars rattle, something rolls across the floor. But neither of us cares.

Nogas kisses me like a drowning man, desperate and reverent, seemingly terrified to stop. His hands are on my waist, my back, my face. My arms circle his neck, pulling him closer until I no longer know where his breath ends and mine begins. My legs wrap around his hips, anchoring my body to his as he devours me without stopping.

We stumble backward into the shelves. The wooden frame groans under our weight, the sound breaking into the still air. One of the lamps flickers, but his body shields me from everything. I feel his heartbeat hammering against mine.

When we finally pull apart, it's not because we want to.

Because we must.

We stop together, gasping, the air trembling between us.

But he doesn't let me go.

Instead, he lowers his head and presses his lips to my hair.

"Please," he rasps. "Let me hold you."

The plea undoes me.

I nod.

He wraps his arms around me slowly. I slide my arms around his waist in return, my cheek against his chest. His breath is uneven, but steadying, and I feel the tension in him slowly ease.

He smooths my hair back from my face, his fingers brushing the flower behind my ear, the one Kala blessed.

"It's crooked," he murmurs, straightening it gently.

"You're impossible," I whisper, voice shaking.

He gives a quiet, hollow laugh. "Maybe. But not for long."

He says nothing more, but I can feel it in his hold.

The truth he's too proud to say.

Not for long.

Not when Tinigbasan waits. Not when Sidlaw's name already hangs like an omen over tomorrow.

He finds my cloak where it fell and wraps it around me, pulling it close. "You should not be cold."

"I'm not," I answer, but he still holds me until I stop shaking.

We end up sitting on the floor amid the scrolls and trinkets, my head against his shoulder as I sort them into piles by kingdom and subject. The light from the oil lamps wavers over us, golden and quiet, as I work.

"These were all from different kingdoms," I tell him, reaching for a scroll lined with wave markings. "Panlawod, Lumbaton, even Tuguran. They send their writings to Tinigbasan, and I share them with the temple. Agdan would always say knowledge should flow like water, so it never dries up."

Nogas traces one of the wooden trinkets on the floor with his thumb. "And you come here every season?"

"Yes." My voice catches a little. "To honor my mother's memory. But not just that. To make sure what we know, the truth of what we've lived, stays safe with people who won't twist it into something to control others. Hamtic has enough kings who use words like weapons."

He looks down at me. "And what do you use, Princess?"

I think about it for a long moment before I answer. "Hope. Even when it hurts to keep it."

He says nothing, just breathes out slowly. The sound is almost a sigh.

The silence that follows feels heavy but warm, the kind that fills a room instead of emptying it. Outside, the night deepens. I feel my body start to sink against his, my eyes growing heavy.

"I'm sleepy, Nogas," I murmur.

He brushes a thumb under my jaw, smiling faintly. "You should rest."

"I don't want the night to end."

"Neither do I, Princess," he answers softly.

"Anini," I tell him. "You can call me that. For as long as we can both speak like this."

I almost tell him that time might not even last until sunrise, but I don't.

He only nods.

"We never did get to complete the rites of servitude," I say instead, running my hands over the scrolls laid out neatly before me, uncertain if I will be here next season to do the same. "I was hoping Agdan could have done it, but without him, we shall have it at Tinigbasan."

"As you wish," he answers. "Anini."

I smile at the sound of my name on his lips, and turn my head up so I can kiss him. He kisses me back without hesitation, only tenderness.

I reach up to smooth his hair. It feels like steel, if steel were soft.

My warrior of the sun.

But the sun will take him from me when it next rises.

I smile at him, trying to make my voice light and carefree. "Did you know Mion used to be my mother's shield? She was the one who made him tell Lira he loved her. I managed to get the story out of Lira one night, but she was too embarrassed to tell it again. My mother was…romantic. I suppose she gets it from Kala and Suba."

For a heartbeat, he says nothing, but then he stands and helps me to my feet. Before he lets my hand go, Nogas presses his lips to my knuckles.

I take a breath to steady myself.

"Wait," I say suddenly, remembering. "Agdan said he kept something special for me before I arrived."

I move toward the far wall, where a tapestry hangs. It's made of woven reeds dyed in blue and gold, depicting the sun over the river. I reach behind it, fingers finding the small carvings set into the stone.

There are seven notches. I twist and push them in sequence, the way Agdan had taught me when I was small.

A faint click echoes through the chamber.

"Here," I say softly. "Help me."

Nogas steps beside me, planting his feet and pressing both hands against the wall. The slab grinds open, revealing a hollow vault inside. The air that escapes is cool, untouched for days.

Inside, there's only a single scroll.

I reach in, confused, and draw it out. The parchment is sealed with wax bearing the mark of the river temple, a coiled serpent biting its tail.

When I unroll it over the table, the ink glimmers faintly in the lamplight.

DUNGOG SANG DUTA, DAGAT, KAG DUGO.

The Honor of Land, Sea, and Blood.

Nogas reads aloud, his voice low.

"In the age before kingdoms were fixed by stone and tide, the rulers of Hamtic decreed that no man could claim a kingdom unless he could prove his worth to the gods themselves. Thus was born the Three Honors."

He glances at me. "This was born of the legend we only heard about before, Princess."

I nod, tracing the edge of the parchment with my fingers. My heart is beating faster now.

There's a smaller parchment folded behind the main scroll, its seal slightly cracked.

The handwriting is Agdan's. I would know it anywhere. They're shapes carved with patience and care.

I read it aloud, my voice a little unsteady.

To my beloved student,
Anini of Tinigbasan,
You were born of the river and the sea, and now you come of age beneath their gaze.
This scroll was passed on to me by the keepers of the temple who found your mother when the sea gave her to the world.
Let this be my gift to you, a true legacy that befits a princess and a scholar such as yourself.
May you never forget that honor is not inherited.
It is always chosen.

The words sink through me like water through sand. My hands tremble slightly as I trace the wax sigil.

Nogas watches me in silence, his eyes curious and thoughtful.

"So he kept it," I say softly. "After all this time. Waiting for me."

He nods. "A promise held until its time."

I swallow hard, looking back down at the bigger scroll. The ink looks older than anything in this room, older than even the temple itself. The temple's history, the land's memory, the gods' own decree…all folded into one.

We unroll the rest of the scroll together. The script is

older now, older than anything I have ever seen, curling like vines across the parchment.

The Rite of Living Land. Let the land remember your heart.

The Rite of Shaping Sea. Let the waves bear your name.

The Rite of Binding Blood. Let your honor flow as the rivers do.

"Three rites," I say. "Three rites to claim a kingdom."

The lines at the bottom of the scroll are written in thicker, darker ink, the words bolder and heavier.

By the land you raise, the sea you tame, and the blood you spill in truth. Let gods and men bear witness now. Honor needs no proof.

Nogas studies the words. I meet his eyes, and for a moment, neither of us speaks. The lamps flicker as if the air itself is holding its breath.

"Suba," he says softly, almost to himself. His gaze stays fixed on the words, the muscles in his jaw tightening. "It makes sense, doesn't it? He carved the mountains to meet the sea. He fought the very world to reach Kala. Maybe these were the rites he fulfilled."

I lean closer to the parchment, tracing the ink where it curls like water. "You think this is how he earned the right to rule beyond the veil?"

Nogas nods slowly. "*The Rite of Binding Blood*, when he challenged the gods and the land itself to prove his strength. *The Rite of Living Land*, when he shaped the earth, carving the path from the mountain to the sea. And *The Rite of Shaping Sea…*" He glances at me, his eyes dark and distant. "That must have been when Kala met him halfway."

I say the words softly, as if afraid to disturb them. "When water and stone made flame."

Nogas glances at me. "He didn't just win her, Princess. He earned her world. That was his kingdom, the realm between earth and water. Not built with walls or crowns, but with love strong enough to break them."

Something in my chest twists. "Then maybe that's why the veil still opens for them. The gods remembered what they did."

"Or what they lost," Nogas says quietly. His hand brushes the scroll, his thumb resting beside mine. "Every rite has a price. Even beyond the veil, that doesn't change."

The thought settles between us, heavy as stone and just as certain.

I stare at the words again, the script pulsing faintly in the light.

By the land you raise, the sea you tame, and the blood you spill in truth. Let gods and men bear witness now. Honor needs no proof.

A shiver runs through me. "You think this…this will happen again?"

Nogas' eyes flick to the door as if he can already see the path waiting beyond it.

"It always does," he says quietly. "The names change, but the rites never end. There will always be someone asked to prove their worth. To fight. To bleed."

"And to love?"

His mouth twists, half a smile, half something else entirely. "Especially to love."

The silence that follows feels almost sacred.

I roll the scroll gently, the parchment whispering against itself, and tie it with a strip of gold thread from a trinket.

"Then if Suba's kingdom was born of these rites," I say softly, "maybe ours is next."

He looks at me, something fierce and unspoken flickering in his eyes. "Maybe it already is."

For a moment, the air seems to hum again, with the same deep thrumming that had filled the springs atop the mountain, where flame met stone.

And in that stillness, I realize that the world isn't waiting for a kingdom to rise.

It's waiting for us to decide what kind it will be.

CHAPTER 24

Road of Change

Nogas

Dawn comes too soon.

The night has been long and sleepless. It's the kind of night that doesn't end, but just changes color. I tried to sleep, but every time I closed my eyes, I saw her face in the lamplight of Agdan's study, her breath still warm against my skin, her hand clutching the ancient scroll as if it were her heart.

So I just decided to stand watch outside her chamber door until the first birds stirred in the trees. It was better than doing nothing.

When the first gold touched the mist, I knew the morning I didn't want had arrived.

The temple is quiet, wrapped in a thin veil of fog. The smell of wet earth and river weed clings to the air. Water beads on the stone pillars, on my cloak, on the shield strapped to my back. The world looks half-awake, the same way I feel.

After speaking with Joru and the Temple Guard about reinforcements from Tinigbasan, Anini moves through the courtyard like a ghost of sunlight, giving orders softly but firmly. The guards and drivers check the carriages; the handmaidens tie the last of the provisions. Lira hovers close to her as always, muttering under her breath.

Then Joru strides toward us from the gates, his voice carrying low urgency. "Princess, there's a royal envoy waiting outside the river path. They bear the colors of Dalidnon."

Dalidnon.

The word hits like a spear to the chest.

Anini's expression barely changes. She draws herself up, every inch the princess. "Tell them to wait. We shall depart once my guards and handmaidens are accounted for."

"Yes, Princess." Joru bows, but I can see tension in his shoulders as he turns back toward the gate.

Beside me, Lira murmurs, "What could they want? To escort us?"

"Or to watch us," I say quietly.

Anini glances at me, but before she can answer, the sound of hurried footsteps echoes through the courtyard. A handmaiden carrying a jar rushes toward us.

"Princess!" she gasps. "Another caravan is coming up the path. The watchman said he recognized their standard. It's Prince Sidlaw. He's here."

My body tenses before my mind catches up.

Sidlaw.

The name itself feels like stone in my mouth.

Before I can think, Joru's voice calls out from the courtyard archway, "Confirmed, Princess! The Prince of Dalidnon approaches with his own guard. They bear the royal crest of the sea kingdom!"

I turn with the others. Through the gray morning light, the banners appear first, blue silk streaked with white foam, bearing the golden seahorse sigil of Dalidnon. Then the riders come into view, armor gleaming, their formation precise.

And at the center, I know on sight it's Prince Sidlaw.

He dismounts before reaching the steps, removing his helm. He looks composed and solemn, the cast of his face almost grave. His long dark hair is bound neatly, his skin sun-marked, his gaze steady as the tide.

When he bows to Anini, he does it deeply, with no hint of arrogance.

"Princess Anini," he says. "When I received word from your father's messenger of the attack, I could not remain idle in Tinigbasan. I rode through the night. I had to see for myself that you were safe."

His voice is smooth, rich, and dignified. The kind of voice that commands both men and silence.

Anini inclines her head. "Prince Sidlaw. Your concern honors me."

He straightens. He appears to be almost my height, and wider across the shoulders.

"It was not concern alone," Sidlaw says. "When I heard

that the river temple was attacked, I thought of Agdan. He was a friend to our court. His loss wounds us all."

Her jaw softens, just slightly. "He was my teacher. His death is…not yet real."

He nods slowly. "Then I share your grief, Princess."

Their eyes meet. And though she hides it well, I feel it. The change in her stance, the stiffness in her shoulders.

This is the man she is promised to. The one she will soon call her equal in name, if not in heart.

Sidlaw gestures toward his own guards and carts. "I bring a small detachment to see you safely to Tinigbasan. My father insisted. He feared another ambush along the border roads."

Anini's voice remains calm. "That won't be necessary. My own men are sufficient. We are capable of defending ourselves."

He smiles faintly, polite but firm. "Forgive me, Princess, but I believe these raiders grow bolder by the day. The road to Tinigbasan is long and treacherous. Allow me the honor of escorting you home."

I can feel the irritation beneath her composure. "Your honor is appreciated. But you need not fear for my safety."

Sidlaw raises an eyebrow. "No?"

Anini turns slightly, and for the first time since dawn, looks at me.

"No," she says. "I have a shield."

Every gaze follows hers.

Sidlaw's eyes settle on me. He looks curious and assessing, but not cruel. "Ah. So this is the warrior of Kalisidlan I've heard so much about."

I bow slightly. "Prince."

He studies me for a moment longer, then says, "Your reputation reached even Dalidnon. They say you fight like the mountain storms themselves."

I meet his gaze evenly. "I serve the Princess of Tinigbasan. Her words are mine to answer."

The faintest shadow of amusement crosses his face. "A loyal man. That is rare."

He turns back to Anini. "You choose your guard well, Princess."

Anini's tone is cool. "I choose those who protect without question."

Sidlaw chuckles softly, though it doesn't reach his eyes. "Then perhaps we shall have the chance to test that loyalty soon enough."

I don't move. I don't speak.

But something in me tightens painfully, deep in my chest.

When he offers his hand to help her up the carriage steps, she hesitates just for a breath. Then she places her hand in his, composed and regal.

I follow behind, silent, my palm tightening around the hilt of my dagger though I know the gesture is useless.

As the caravan begins to roll, the wheels grinding softly over the damp earth, Sidlaw rides beside her carriage window. He speaks to her through the curtain, his voice low and courteous. She answers with careful grace.

And I walk beside the wheel on the opposite side, every step a vow I can't speak aloud.

To protect her.

Even from what she might become.

Even from what I already feel.

Ahead, the road bends east toward Tinigbasan.

Toward her father.

Toward everything that waits to break whatever fragile truth we found in the dark.

I do not look back.

But I know that if I did, the river would still be watching.

CHAPTER 25

Anini

The road to Tinigbasan stretches before us in a veil of mist.

The river follows us for a while, glinting silver through the trees before vanishing behind the hills.

Dalidnon's banners ride ahead, their blue and white edges rippling in the wind. Behind us the handmaidens ride, their silks veiled against dust and sun.

Prince Sidlaw rides at my side.

He is not the boy I remember. Gone is the brash, quick-tempered heir with the sharp tongue and sharper pride. This man is quietly composed, his face all solemn angles in the early morning light. His long hair is tied back, his jaw roughened by the faint shadow of travel. The light armor of Dalidnon fits him like a second skin, and a bow rests against his saddle, its string humming softly when the wind ripples through the caravan.

He looks…older. And far wiser.

"Your journey must have been long and tiring," I say finally. "You need not have come yourself."

Sidlaw turns his head slightly, the sunlight catching in his eyes.

"When I heard you were attacked, I thought of my mother," he says. "She told me once, if you care for someone's safety, don't send a messenger. Go yourself. And the greatest rulers I met on my travels taught me the same. There is no stronger blade than your own will and heart."

His tone is soft, without boast or pretense. It almost disarms me.

"I didn't expect you to be a man of philosophy," I say lightly.

"Once I wasn't," he admits. "Once I thought war could build kingdoms. Now I think it only buries them. A strong blade is not meant to fight, but to protect."

He looks forward again, the lines of his face softened by thought. "I read now, when I can. Study. Travel. You'd be surprised what scrolls the kingdoms beyond the isles keep hidden away."

That makes me smile despite myself. "You collect scrolls?"

"I do," he says, glancing sidelong at me. "Not as many as you, I imagine. I've heard of your visits to the river temple, exchanging scrolls and knowledge with Shaman Agdan."

My throat tightens a little at his name. "He was…family."

Sidlaw nods respectfully. "Then his loss is ours as well."

Lira is seated on my other side, her posture stiff, eyes flicking between us like a hawk's. She clears her throat. "The Prince of Dalidnon seems to have learned diplomacy. How refreshing."

Sidlaw only smiles faintly. "Perhaps I have learned to listen more since my youth, Lady Lira. To hear what others have to say, above all."

Lira raises an eyebrow, but Sidlaw doesn't rise to the bait. Instead, he adjusts the reins of his water beast and falls silent, the picture of calm patience.

I find myself unnerved. Who is this man?

Beside us, Nogas walks with my guards, steps silent and precise, his face unreadable. He hasn't spoken much since dawn. His spear gleams against his shoulder, and the golden shield Suba gifted him catches the light like a fragment of the sun. Every movement of his is controlled, but I can feel the storm just beneath his skin.

He moves as if he's holding the world together by sheer will. And I can't look at him for too long without feeling like I'm breaking something sacred.

The morning burns into noon. The mist has lifted. The air grows heavy and bright, the kind that makes everything too real.

Sidlaw slows his mount and calls out, "Princess, it's nearly midday. The guards and beasts will need rest. May we stop by the river bend for the meal?"

I nod. "We'll take an hour."

The caravan halts. Handmaidens climb down to spread blankets beneath the trees, bringing baskets of fruit and bread and jugs of water. I stand, brushing dust from my skirts, and reach for the edge of the carriage. Sidlaw dismounts first and moves to help me down.

But I lift my chin and call, "Nogas."

He's there in an instant.

For a breath, the world narrows to the space between us. His eyes meet mine. The look in them is unguarded, aching. The sound of the river, the creak of saddles, the low hum of men's voices…all of it fades.

It's only his eyes of river stone.

He offers his hand and I take it. His palm is as calloused and warm as I remember.

When he helps me down, the contact burns.

"Thank you," I say softly.

"Princess," he answers, bowing slightly.

But before I can take another step, his expression changes, the careful tenderness becoming fierce urgency.

Then he slams into me.

"DOWN!" he shouts, his body covering mine as the air splits with the hiss of arrows.

The world erupts.

The first volley strikes the carriages, splintering wood and sending the beasts screaming. The handmaidens cry out, scattering for cover. Guards raise their shields, but the second wave follows, arrows streaking through the trees like black fire.

"Raiders!" Nogas roars, rolling off me, already drawing his spear.

Sidlaw's bow is in his hands in a blink, his first arrow flying before his mount even rears. "To arms! Protect the princess!"

I scramble to my knees, mud biting my hands. Through the chaos, I see them, figures slipping from the forest, their bodies wrapped in moss and bark, faces painted in dark green streaks.

The Dumalog.

But there's something else behind them. Darker shapes, their armor glinting black and red like dried blood.

Nogas freezes mid-strike.

"Kalisidlan," he breathes.

My heart stops. "What? Why would your own—"

"I don't know," he growls, parrying a blade with his shield, "but the prisoner at the temple spoke truth. There's a pact between them!"

"Then they…"

"Came for you, Princess!"

The first wave of raiders cuts us off. Nogas lunges forward, spear flashing, catching two raiders through the chest. Sidlaw moves to my side, his blade drawn now, cutting down a Dumalog who gets too close.

"Behind the carriages!" Sidlaw orders. "Form the line!"

Nogas' voice carries over the din. "Shields to the front! Protect the princess and the prince!"

Our remaining guards lock into formation, forming a wall of shields and blades. Nogas stands at the head, his golden shield glinting through the smoke and sunlight, deflecting arrow after arrow.

"Hold!" he shouts.

The air is chaos. Fire arrows streak through the trees, catching the brush aflame. The smell of burning moss and blood fills my lungs.

I see one of my handmaidens fall, her cries echoing through the trees. Lira grabs a dagger from the ground, slashing at a raider who lunges toward us.

Nogas drives his spear into another, then takes a hit to the shoulder but doesn't falter. He turns his head toward me.

And that's when the second arrow finds him.

It strikes deep, just below his ribs.

"NOGAS!" I scream. "NO!"

I run forward, grabbing a fallen guard's dagger, but Lira pulls me back. "Princess! Stay back!"

Sidlaw is bleeding, too, a dagger lodged in his arm, but he still fights, his blade moving like firelight.

Nogas stumbles as he pulls out the arrows, one knee to the ground, blood soaking his tunic.

"Sidlaw!" he gasps, crawling forward. "Take her! Take the princess!"

Sidlaw grabs his own wounded arm, snarling through his teeth. "I won't leave you!"

"You must, Prince," Nogas insists, coughing blood. "Run. Run to Tinigbasan! We'll hold them!"

Lira's eyes are wild, desperate. "Yes, my Prince, go! Take her!"

Sidlaw turns, grabbing me by the arm, his strength unreal despite his wounds.

"No!" I cry. "No! I'm not running!"

Nogas pushes to his feet, blood streaming down his arm as he raises his shield. "I'll cover you! Go!"

Another wave surges forward, and Nogas meets them head-on, shield flashing gold.

As Sidlaw drags me away from the battle and tries to pull

his water beast along, Lira disappears into the smoke, blades in both hands. Her scream blends with the clash of steel.

Nogas turns to me, eyes finding mine.

"I love you, Princess," he tells me softly. "It has been my greatest honor to be yours. I will die in your name, as I promised."

Then he smiles.

And an arrow takes him in the chest.

"NO!" I thrash against Sidlaw's hold, but he hauls me up and spurs the beast forward, and we break through the smoke.

The world blurs.

Fire and blood. The roar of steel and death. All of it.

Just a blur.

There is only Nogas.

The last thing I see is the sun catching the edge of his golden shield, his body still standing, spear lifted as if to strike the sky itself.

Then he is gone.

CHAPTER 26

King of Blood

Nogas

THE ARROW HITS ME CLEAN THROUGH THE CHEST.

It's the sound that gets me first. Not the pain, not even the breath leaving my body, but that dry, cracking sound as it splits flesh and bone, lodging deep enough through the armor that I can feel my heart shudder against it.

Then comes the silence.

Through the blur of dust and fire, I see Anini disappearing down the forest path, the beast beneath her pounding through the smoke, Sidlaw gripping the reins with one arm, blood pouring down the other.

Her hair catches the light as they vanish between the trees, and for one impossible moment, I think she turns her head back toward me.

I tell her with my heart what I can no longer say with my lips.

I love you, Anini.

You are the vow I choose.

The only vow I will keep choosing.

For all eternity.

Then she is gone.

The pain flares in my chest, but I barely feel it. Pain has always been my oldest companion, my first memory, my first teacher. Pain forged me when I had no name, no family, no peace.

Pain is nothing.

But she...

She is everything.

Everything worth bleeding for.

Everything worth dying for.

I stagger, my breath shallow. The arrow is of Kalisidlan make, its steel strong enough to pierce the armor of lowlanders. My hand finds the shaft of the arrow and grips it, but I don't pull it free. Not yet. I drop the golden shield to the ground, grab a fallen Dalidnon blade slick with blood, and with one slice, I shear off the arrow's shaft close to my chest. The world tilts, black around the edges, but the pressure eases enough for me to move.

I lift the shield again, my arm trembling, and raise my spear. The heat of the burning trees claws at my skin, smoke filling my lungs. The roar of men and fire merge into one.

And then I run.

Straight into the storm.

The spear moves like a living thing in my hands. The first Dumalog doesn't even see me coming before his throat opens. The second swings an axe. I duck, twist, drive my knee into his stomach, and slam the butt of my spear through his skull.

Blood sprays across my face. I barely notice.

"FOR THE PRINCESS!" I shout.

The words tear through the battlefield like a call to gods who have long stopped listening. But I don't care. I fight for her. For her name. For the way she said mine as if it meant something.

Spear. Shield. Roar.

Again. Again. Again.

The Dumalog fall like waves breaking on rock. The men of Kalisidlan, the ones who should have been my brothers, come next. Their armor flashes red and black, the marks of the place I called home.

But I don't slow.

One slashes my shoulder. I pivot, driving my spear under his ribs. Another charges from behind. I spin, letting the shield slam against his jaw. I can taste iron on my tongue, can feel the warmth of blood seeping through my tunic, but I keep going.

Fight until she's free.

Fight until she lives.

I am her shield.

My life is hers.

The world narrows to steel and blood. The roar in my ears becomes the ocean itself. I don't know how long I fight, only that every heartbeat feels borrowed, every swing a promise.

When the last raider falls, I realize I can't feel my legs. My knees hit the ground hard.

Beneath me, the earth runs red.

Mine, theirs, everyone's.

Hers.

I can hear her name in my head, faint, like wind through reeds.

Anini.

Then, through the haze, I hear another voice.

"Nogas!"

I turn my head. Lira's limping through the smoke, her arm bleeding, her robe torn and burned at the edges. She stumbles past the dead, past the flames, until she drops to her knees beside me.

"Is the princess safe?" she gasps, grabbing my shoulders. "Did you see them leave?"

I cough, a warm trail of blood spilling down my chin. "Yes…Lady Lira. I saw her go. With the prince. Toward Tinigbasan."

She exhales, the sound halfway between a sob and a laugh. "Then it's enough. It meant something. What we did here. It meant everything if she lives."

Her hand is on my cheek for only a moment before she collapses next to me, too weak to rise.

The flames crackle louder. The sky spins. The air tastes of iron and death.

And then I see them.

Figures moving through the haze, tall and armored, too slow to be headed for battle. The colors of Kalisidlan. The crest on their cloaks. The flame sigils of the mountain tribes.

Bantawan.

My chieftain.

He strides through the dead, his face half-shadowed by soot. Behind him walks another man, older and white-haired, robed in indigo, his presence cold and heavy as stone.

The soldiers part for them.

"Shaman Oran," Bantawan says. "He's here."

The older man nods, voice deep as thunder. "But the princess has fled."

"It matters not," Bantawan replies. "We have what we came for."

Their eyes turn toward me.

I try to lift my spear, but my body refuses. My arms are shaking. My lungs ache for air.

"He's blessed," Oran says, kneeling beside me, his hand almost gentle on my shoulder. "That shield he bears carries the favor of gods your people never prayed to."

Bantawan folds his arms. "It would seem he did not pray, Shaman. He fought."

"He did," Oran says quietly. "And now he is right where he belongs."

Bantawan studies me for a long time, then turns to his men. "Take him. Tend to his wounds. Then care for the others. Ours and theirs alike. This battle is over."

Oran's head tilts thoughtfully.

"No, Chieftain," he murmurs as he rises, eyes gleaming through the smoke. "It has only begun."

Bantawan lowers his head slightly. "As you say, Shaman. As you say."

The one called Oran looks down at me, voice low when he speaks again.

"Our king has returned. Long live the rightful king of the seas."

The men around us echo the words, a rumble that shakes the burning ground.

"Long live the king."

As darkness pulls me under, I swear I hear the river answering back.

CHAPTER 27

Loss of Light

ANINI

THE ROAD FEELS ENDLESS.

Every jolt on the uneven ground is an echo of battle. Every shaky breath I take sounds like a heartbeat that stopped too soon.

Sidlaw steers the beast like a man gone mad, blood still staining his arm where the arrows found him, his posture unflinching. I sit as the trees and wind roar around us, clutching the saddle, lost and empty.

By the time the gates of Tinigbasan rise from the fog, the world feels hollow.

The guards shout our arrival. Servants rush forward, voices rising with disbelief and shock all at once. I slide down from the beast, caught by handmaidens and nurses, numb, and Datu Oyong is already there.

My father.

My ruler.

The reason I will soon be bound.

His face collapses with grief and relief the moment he sees me.

"Anini!" he cries, rushing forward. He takes my face between his trembling hands. "By the gods! You're alive! You're safe!"

"I am, Father," I hear myself say. "But the others…"

I can't finish. I don't need to.

Oyong's eyes flick toward the blood on my sleeves, the torn hem of my robe, the empty space where Nogas, Lira, and my court should have been.

Behind him stands Datu Radul of Dalidnon, broad and regal. His expression is grave, though his eyes settle on his son, and I see both worry and pride there.

Radul inclines his head to me. "Your courage honors your mother's name, Princess."

"Your warriors fought bravely, Datu," Sidlaw says to my father, his voice steady. "They held the line until the end. The Dumalog and Kalisidlan will not recover easily from what happened by the river."

Oyong's hand grips mine tightly. "At what cost?"

Sidlaw looks away. "Too many."

I feel the words like a blade twisting in my chest.

Lira.

Nogas.

Their names burn behind my eyes, but no sound comes.

The palace is too quiet.

Seven days pass like the space between breaths. I wake, eat when I remember to, and stare at the library windows until the light dies. Servants move like ghosts. Even the sea seems quieter, the tides respectful of my silence.

I am half-alive, drifting between sleep and memory. The court whispers that I am mourning. They do not know how small that word feels.

When the seventh day is almost over, I call for Mion.

He arrives quickly, his armor polished, his eyes soft but careful. I am seated by the low tables, scrolls that I cannot read laid open before me.

"I'm sorry, Mion," I say, the words scraping my throat raw. "For Lira."

He bows low. "We serve the kingdom, Princess. We have always been ready for the sacrifices it calls on us."

"I know," I say. "But I still should have—"

He interrupts gently. "You survived. That is all that matters. Lira would say the same, perhaps a little more forcefully."

I look at him, but all I can see is the blood on the ground, the way Nogas took the arrows and kept standing. The way Lira told me to run, and ran into battle to save me.

Mion lowers his gaze.

"I am also sorry, Princess," he says, his voice almost breaking, "for what happened to Shaman Agdan…and to Nogas."

The name cuts through me like lightning.

"Yes," I say softly. "Nogas."

My throat tightens, but I force the words out. They tumble from my lips painfully. "He was everything a shield should be…and more. This kingdom didn't deserve him. No one deserves him. Except the gods. He was greater than all of us."

Mion bows again, wordlessly. When I finally dismiss him, he leaves without a sound.

I look at the scrolls in front of me, and think of the ancient scroll from Agdan. I kept it safely in the shaman's vault before leaving the temple, but it doesn't matter now.

Honor is not inherited, he'd written to me. *It is always chosen.*

But there is nothing left to choose.

There is only duty.

And loss.

Not long after, a handmaiden appears by the library door, pale and hesitant.

"Princess," she murmurs, "Prince Sidlaw requests an audience. He says he'll leave if you refuse."

I close the scroll in front of me, though I haven't been reading it. "No. I'll see him."

She bows and departs.

When Sidlaw enters, he moves quietly. He looks tired, his arm still bound in clean linen, his dark hair loose around his shoulders. He's dressed simply, no armor. Just a man, carrying a small carved box in his hands.

"Princess," he says softly. "Forgive the intrusion. I only wanted to see how you fare…and to say I'm deeply sorry. For your losses. For your nurse. And your shield."

He hesitates, then opens the box. Inside, nestled on a fold of silk, lies the flower Kala had blessed, the white and yellow bloom that once shone behind my ear.

"I found this," Sidlaw says as he lowers the box next to my scrolls. "It fell when we reached Tinigbasan. I've never seen its like before. It's beautiful. What is it called?"

For a moment, I can't speak. When my voice finally comes out, it's barely above a whisper.

"River-meets-the-sun. It's…a gift. A token." My voice cracks as my fingers brush the petals. "A memento."

The word shatters something inside me.

The air collapses. The silence breaks.

For the first time since the battle, the tears fall.

They come without sound at first, then with quiet, breaking gasps that tear through my chest. I clutch the flower to my heart, my shoulders shaking.

Sidlaw reaches for me before I collapse to the floor. The flower spills onto the mats next to me.

And then I am crying.

Not weeping, not silent tears, but *sobbing*. My body shakes, the sound raw and trembling, rising from somewhere deep inside.

Sidlaw holds me against him, arms steady, not saying a word. I clutch his tunic, burying my face in his shoulder.

"I should have saved them," I choke. "I should have gone back."

"You couldn't," he says quietly, his hand brushing the back of my head. "No one could have."

"Lira told me to run…but I should have fought. I could fight. I am not helpless…"

Sidlaw doesn't say anything, but his arms tighten around me.

"I saw him fall." My voice tremble. "I saw him *smile*, Sidlaw. As if dying for me was enough."

"It was enough for him, Anini. Because it was you."

That makes me sob harder.

"You've carried the weight of every life in this kingdom since you were born," he continues. "Let someone hold you this once."

And I do. I let him.

I cry until my voice is gone, until my throat aches and my breath comes in small, uneven bursts.

Sidlaw doesn't let go. He just stays there, the two of us on the library floor, surrounded by the scent of old paper and loss.

When the worst of it passes, I say, "They gave everything. And I'm still here."

Sidlaw carefully brushes a tear from my cheek.

"Then live, Princess," he says. "Live for them."

Outside, the sea wind sighs against the walls. The last light of day filters through the windows, pale gold on the flower lying before me.

River-meets-the-sun.

And for the first time since the battle, I breathe.

CHAPTER 28

Pull of the Past

Nogas

The first thing I feel is the sea breathing. It breathes in and out through the woven walls around me, patient and alive. The air is warm, damp with salt. I hear birds calling over waves, the kind that fly close to water, their cries lonely as if they mourn.

When I open my eyes, I see light moving across a ceiling of reed and wood. The world sways gently beneath me. I'm lying on a bed of woven mats and furs, my body bandaged tight from shoulder to ribs.

It takes me a moment to remember how to breathe.

The battle.

The fire.

Her voice calling my name.

Then the sound of beast hooves thundering down the forest path.

Anini.

I lurch up, dizzy and gasping. Pain lances through my chest and I choke, clutching at the bindings.

"Lie down."

The voice is deep and steady. A hand presses against my shoulder with surprising strength.

"You have been unconscious for three days," the man says. "If you rise too quickly, you'll undo what little healing the sea has granted you."

My vision clears. He sits cross-legged beside me, robes the color of midnight fog, hair white and long, bound behind him. His skin bears markings, lines and swirls in black and deep brown, inked waves circling flame. His eyes are the pale gray of dawn before the sun touches it.

"Who are you?" My voice is rough, raw from thirst.

"I am Oran," he says. "Shaman of the Dumalog."

The name hits like a wave to the ribs.

Dumalog. Raiders. The tide-born enemies of Tinigbasan and all of Hamtic.

I look around, expecting stone prisons or stakes, but the hut is…beautiful.

Everything here glows with light and care. Polished coral beams arch like ribs, sea glass dangles from the ceiling, catching sunlight in gentle hues. The floor is white sand strewn with shells. Through the window I see other huts rising over water, with wood bridges connecting small islands wreathed in mist.

"This is…Dumalog?"

"It is," Oran replies simply. "The heart of the isles."

"I thought these islands were ash," I say. "Destroyed by storms or by war."

A faint smile crosses his lips. "So their kingdoms told you."

He reaches for a jug, pours clear water into a shell cup, and hands it to me. I drink greedily. The water tastes faintly sweet.

"What do you want from me?" I ask. "Why save me?"

Oran studies me for a long time. "Because I knew your name long before you spoke it. Because your fate was written before you were born."

I frown. "Prophecies and riddles. I'm no believer in such things."

He chuckles. "Belief is irrelevant, boy. Truth does not vanish because you doubt it."

I try to stand, but pain folds me in half. "If this is truth, then tell me. Why am I here? What do you mean you knew me?"

Oran leans forward, elbows resting on his knees. "You were told you were a child of Kalisidlan, yes? An orphan raised by the chief as his warrior?"

"Yes."

"Then you were told only half the story."

I narrow my eyes. "And you claim to know the rest?"

"I do," he says. "Because I was there when it began."

Something in his tone, quiet yet deeply burdened, roots me in place.

He looks past me, toward the window, where the tide glitters gold. "Many sun-cycles ago, before Datu Oyong's reign, the kingdom of Tinigbasan had another ruler. His father, Murong. A man who built peace through fear, and fear through silence. He trusted no one, not even those who spoke for the gods."

I stay quiet.

"There was a young oracle then," Oran continues. "Her name was Saraya. She was of Tinigbasan blood, blessed by visions of the river and the sea. She saw things the Datu did not wish to hear. That his kingdom, the jewel of the isles, would fall not to storm or sword, but to love. That the river would meet the sun, and that new blood, born of the sea, would rise to reclaim the land."

I shake my head slowly. "Love? That's what he feared?"

The old man smiles without warmth. "Men in power fear many things, boy. Love is merely the name they give to what they cannot control."

He stands, pacing toward the open door, his shadow long across the sand. "Murong called it blasphemy. He said no sea-born child could bear the favor of the gods. So he ordered Saraya silenced. Permanently."

My pulse quickens. "What happened to her?"

"She fled," Oran says quietly. "Because I helped her."

My breath catches. "You?"

"Yes." His gaze meets mine, and for the first time, I see it, the ache of memory in the lines of his face. "I loved her. I was a scribe of the Tinigbasan temple in my youth. I saw the storm in her visions, and I chose to walk through it with her. We escaped the capital, crossed the rivers, and fled to the open sea."

His voice softens. "She was already carrying our child."

The silence that follows is unbearable. The shaman's hands tremble slightly as he continues.

"But the sea is cruel. She labored for days under a moonless sky. The child came too soon. She gave me a daughter. Then the tide took her."

I can't look away. "What happened to the child?"

"She was swept away," Oran says. "Lost to the waves. I searched until my bones bled, until I could no longer tell the difference between the stars and her mother's eyes. I failed them both."

The words hang between us like the smoke of too many forgotten fires.

After a long pause, I say, "Then you turned to Dumalog."

He nods. "The sea took everything from me, and so I gave myself to it. I don't even know how I still lived after all that had happened. The people here found me adrift, nearly dead. They took me in. I became their shaman, their voice when they had none."

He takes a deep breath. "Sun-cycles later, I heard whispers. A child found at sea by mermaids and delivered to the river temple. A girl raised by scholars. Oyong, then the second son, loved her since he first laid eyes on her. The girl was named Rumina. She became Dayang of Tinigbasan once the crown passed to Oyong."

The name slams into me like thunder.

"Rumina," I echo.

"Yes." His eyes glisten now, not with light but with memory. "Your princess' mother. My daughter."

I can't breathe.

My hands grip the edge of the mat until the woven reeds creak. "You're saying Anini—"

"Is the child of my child," he finishes softly. "The river's jewel, born of a line blessed by the sea. And you, Nogas…" He steps closer, his gaze piercing. "You are the other half of what Saraya saw."

I shake my head violently. "No. I'm no one's heir. I'm a soldier. A weapon. That's all I've ever been."

"You were born to Rigo," Oran says. "The last chief of Dumalog, slain when Murong's armies burned these isles. His last act was to save you, his only child, by sending you north to Kalisidlan. To grow where the sun could temper the sea in your blood. I was the one who brought you to Bantawan himself."

My heart stops. "Rigo…" The name feels strange on my tongue, and yet it burns like a memory I've always carried.

"Dumalog was never born of piracy or war," he continues. "We were exiles. Fisherfolk and seafarers who refused to bow. Traders who refused to pay tribute. Survivors of Hamtic's attempts at conquest of the smaller isles. So the kingdoms of the coast called us rebels, thieves, raiders. They hunted us. Rigo kept us alive for as long as he could fight. He was the true king of the sea. He welcomed and sheltered all, even the people and kin of his enemies. Just as the sea does."

Rebels. Raiders.

Hunted.

The words spin in my head, but Oran keeps speaking, and I listen.

"The sea remembers its own. So does prophecy. I saw Saraya again, long after her death. She came to me in the tides, her voice bound to foam and wind. She said, *Two children will bring forth water and flame from stone. They will make the river and sea meet, and the world will be remade."*

He kneels before me, eyes shining. *"A jewel of the river. A warrior of the sun. Both with the sea in their blood."*

The air now feels too thick to breathe.

"I'm…" My throat tightens. "You're saying I am…"

"The son of Rigo," the old man rasps. "Heir to Dumalog. Blood of the sea, forged in sunlight."

I stare at him, the world lurching around me.

Everything I thought I knew—my clan, my oath, even my name—feels like a lie carved into someone else's skin.

"I don't want this," I say hoarsely. "I didn't ask for it. I don't want thrones, or crowns, or prophecy."

He nods slowly. "No one ever does. But blood remembers even when the heart refuses."

I stare at him, questions still swirling in my head. "If Agdan was the man who raised your daughter, then why did your people kill him? He was loyal to the gods, to the river. He protected Rumina when others would have used her."

His eyes close, the faint light tracing the deep lines of his face. "Loyalty and blindness often share the same face."

He turns to the window, watching the waves. "Agdan was a scholar of faith. He believed that if the old prophecies threatened peace, then it was his duty to bury them. He thought he could keep balance by silencing truth."

I frown. "Silencing truth?"

"He feared what Saraya saw," Oran says quietly. "He believed that if the blood of the sea ever mixed again with the blood of the river, it would destroy Tinigbasan. So he erased every record of her words, every trace of her name, every whisper of the prophecy. But it was already too late."

"He did it to protect the kingdom," I say.

"Yes," he agrees, voice darkening. "And in doing so, he chained it. He made peace into a cage and called it faith. That is what made him dangerous."

He looks at me then, his gaze unwavering. "The Dumalog did not strike to conquer. We struck to remind the river that the sea can never be chained."

I clench my fists. "You call murder…a reminder?"

His voice drops, grave and certain. "When the river dammed the tide, the tide broke the dam. It is nature, boy."

Silence settles between us. The waves outside whisper and break, over and over.

I think of Anini, her wisdom and her strength. I think of Agdan's frail body lying cold at the temple.

"He loved her," I say at last.

"Yes," says Oran. "And that love was real. But love is not always right. Agdan loved Rumina as a father, but he loved Tinigbasan more. He could never accept that his devotion to the kingdom was what doomed her mother—and now, her child."

I swallow hard. "Anini had no choice in any of this."

"She never had one," he says softly. "Agdan tried to silence the tide once. Do you think her Datu father will not do the same when the waves begin to rise again? He has already begun by binding her to the prince of Dalidnon."

His words strike deep, heavy as the sea itself.

I look at the horizon, at the pale shimmer of water. I feel it in my bones. The pull between the river and the tide.

"I don't know what to do in face of all this," I murmur. "I don't even know who I am."

The shaman smiles sadly. "You are what Agdan would never let be born. A man of two truths, and one impossible choice."

I push myself up, staggering to the doorway. The sea stretches before me, endless and alive, the sun spilling molten gold across the waves.

"Then what would you have me do?" I ask softly, as if speaking to the tide.

Oran moves to stand beside me, his voice almost distant when he speaks.

"You find the river, boy. You find her. And when the river meets the sun again, you decide whether you will rise. Or burn. Perhaps this time, you will get to choose your fate."

I stare at the water until my eyes sting. The tide reaches for the shore, retreating only to return.

It feels like breathing. Like fate.

Like her.

CHAPTER 29

Memory of the Heart

Anini

IT HAS BEEN HALF A MOON SINCE THE AMBUSH.

Half a moon of dreaming of the river burning red. Half a moon of waking up screaming in the dead of night.

When I woke this morning, I realized I could not remember the sound of his heartbeat.

I now know only of its silence.

The handmaidens move quietly around me as they braid my hair and layer my robes. My court wear feels heavier, as though every thread remembers something I have forgotten how to carry. The silk on my skin feels beautiful yet suffocating.

On the woven mats near my bed lies Nogas' cloak. Folded, dark, and thick, still faintly smelling of leaves and steel. The maidens never touch it. They tend my chambers as if it were part of the floor, an unspoken boundary between life and the ghost that lingers.

I kneel beside it and touch the edge of the fabric.

But the world still feels cold, even beneath the sun.

Before I leave, I reach up and touch the flower tucked into my hair, the one blessed by Lady Kala.

River-meets-the-sun.

It feels lighter than air, warmer than light.

A memento.

A story that is no longer mine.

Outside, the courtyard glimmers with morning light. Sidlaw waits by the steps of my palace, armor polished, bow strapped across his back. He bows when he sees me, the gesture precise but softened by the look in his eyes.

"Princess," he says, offering his arm. "The Datu awaits in the great hall."

"Thank you," I answer. My voice sounds far away, as if spoken by someone else.

As we walk the stone paths to my father's palace, the brown and gold banners lining the bridges and terraces ripple with the wind. I remember when they used to make me proud. Now they just remind me of what I had—and never got to keep.

Sidlaw walks beside me, his stride even, his presence steady. He doesn't fill the silence with empty comfort. He never does.

"You've seemed distant," he says finally, his voice quiet. "But I understand. Grief is…not an enemy that can be slain."

"I'm not grieving," I answer. "I'm remembering."

He looks at me, his gaze gentle. "Then let me help you remember better days."

I meet his eyes briefly, then look away. "You already have."

He hesitates, then says, "I shall be your shield, Princess. Your shelter and your home, if you let me."

I stop walking. The words hang between us, warm and aching.

He doesn't take them back.

Sidlaw is not the boy I once knew, a youth loud and proud, always chasing victory. Now he speaks like someone who has lost and learned. The calm in his eyes frightens me more than his arrogance ever did.

Since my return, he's visited every day. He reads to me when I let him. He brings scrolls and trinkets and flowers I forget to thank him for. Sometimes he leaves food outside my door when I forget to eat. I never ask him to stay, and he never asks to.

But he is always there.

My father visits often, too, bringing news of the temple and the survivors.

The Dumalog raids continue at our borders.

The Kalisidlan banners have been seen among their ranks.

No envoys have returned.

It is war now.

And Nogas…

Nogas is gone.

So is Lira.

But both bodies have yet to be found.

My father told me Sidlaw himself had proposed to the court to give Nogas the funeral rites of a true warrior of Hamtic, in both the colors of Tinigbasan and Dalidnon. Sidlaw had said he saw Nogas fall, arrows piercing his body. He'd said Nogas bought our escape with his own life.

Sidlaw had said everything with reverence, not pity.

I had no words to give back to my father, Sidlaw, or anyone.

I only had silence.

Three sunsets ago, I attended Lira's ceremonial rites. She'd been given full court honors. Mion and their son did not cry. Neither did I.

Lira would have been embarrassed at such a common display.

Now, as I approach the Datu's hall, my heart drums too fast. I don't want to enter. I don't want to see what this world looks like without him in it.

But I must.

The doors open. The hall feels bigger than I remember. It seems brighter, but emptier. Golden light filters through the shell windows, dancing over carved pillars and banners of every kingdom under the isles. The air is filled with the voices of rulers and envoys.

My father rises from his seat as I walk over to join him. He is dressed in ceremonial robes lined with heavy gold. I know now this is no mere gathering.

"My daughter," he says, voice loud enough to fill the hall, "the Jewel of the Isles returns to stand with her kin."

The courtiers bow.

I bow lower.

Oyong's tone hardens as he addresses the gathering. "You all know the crimes committed against our people. The attack on the princess, twice, and the death of Shaman Agdan of the river temple are acts of war. The isles of Hamtic have united. We will not bow to those who rise from the mud and call it destiny."

My father steps to the center of the hall, his voice rising a little. "As we speak, Datu Radul of Dalidnon has generously dispatched his finest fleet to Dumalog, to make them answer to their crimes."

A murmur ripples through the hall. I hear approval, anger, and pride.

But I feel nothing.

Then Datu Radul joins my father, his sea-blue cloak lined in gold and white glittering as he moves.

"My brothers," he declares, "this war shall show the world that the kingdoms of Hamtic stand together. But unity cannot be words alone. It must be bound by blood, by faith, by family."

He gestures toward me, smiling. "What greater symbol of unity could there be than a bond between the Jewel of the Isles and the Prince of the Sea?"

The hall erupts into murmurs again, louder this time.

Oyong inclines his head solemnly. "We are honored by your proposal, Datu Radul."

Radul turns to Sidlaw. "My son."

Sidlaw takes a deep breath, then moves to face me and my father.

I feel the air ripple around me, with heat, attention, and the weight of every gaze.

Servants in white and blue Dalidnon robes file in, one after another, carrying chests and trays laden with gifts. There are twelve in all.

Silks of Dalidnon blue, pearls strung like tears, carved coral bracelets, a crown of gold, a mirror framed with shells, vials of scented oil, an ivory comb, a sword etched with waves, a bow carved from willow, jars of honeyed wine, a shining cloak of silver thread, and a single, small, golden cup.

Each one is set before me in silence.

Then Sidlaw kneels.

When he speaks, his voice is steady, pitched low in deference.

"Princess Anini, your courage is the dawn that breaks my pride. In your presence, I learned peace. In your wisdom, I saw strength. You are the river, as clear, fierce, and true as the eternal currents. Let me be the sea that embraces and shelters you."

The hall stills.

He looks up at me, and the tenderness in his eyes is almost unbearable.

"It would bring honor to Dalidnon and all of Hamtic," Sidlaw says, "if you were to become my wife. Let the river come home to the sea, and let the waves bear your name."

He bows his head. "I ask not for duty, Princess. I ask for faith. Faith that I will never fail you. That is my vow."

I cannot move.

I cannot breathe.

Sidlaw's words echo through me like a song I don't know the meaning of. Beautiful, but hollow.

I feel their gazes on me.

My father. The courts of Hamtic. The world.

But all I hear is the sound of rain on stone, in a courtyard razed by flames.

All I see is the man whose eyes remind me of river stones, whose embrace made me believe there is hope when there is nothing left but truth.

But that story is no longer mine.

The flower in my hair seems to tremble in the wake of that emptiness.

And I hear my own voice answer, distant and fragile. "Yes."

The word falls out of me like ash.

"Yes, it would be my honor."

I see relief and joy and triumph in the faces around me, but I don't hear their cheers.

This time, all I hear is the whisper of the currents.

Then…

The flower slips from my hair.

It lands softly on the floor, still impossibly whole and beautiful, petals spreading like sunlight spilled across water.

Five rays ignite, pure white and blinding, bursting outward in a pulse that shakes the hall. Light fills the air, warm and alive.

It feels like the heart of the sun rising beneath the sea.

And I fall to my knees.

The world blurs. My vision dissolves into gold. A sound echoes through me, not heard, but felt.

A heartbeat, strong and steady.

His.
The hall fades.
The noise dies.
And in that silence, I know.
Nogas.
He's alive.

CHAPTER 30

Waves of War

Nogas

SEVEN DAYS.

The sea has kept me alive for seven days.

Seven dawns of salt and breath and pain.

The wounds on my chest are knitting shut, the skin raw but healing. When I breathe, it feels like fire and foam, but it no longer burns the way it used to. The Dumalog healers say it's a good sign.

I don't know what *"good"* means anymore.

The village stretches across eight islets joined by bridges of wood, rope, and coral. Children run barefoot on the sandbars. Women wade through shallows to collect shells. Men dive with nets woven by their own hands. It's a kingdom without walls, and yet every soul here stands guard over the other.

Sometimes I forget they were called raiders. They look more like survivors who simply learned to stop bowing.

Oran visits me every morning. He says it's to check my wounds, but I think it's to see if the sea hasn't decided to take me back.

He always begins the day with silence, letting the sound of waves do the talking. I've learned more from his silence than from most men's words.

By the seventh morning, I am allowed to walk beyond my hut.

The sand burns beneath my bare feet. The tide laps at my ankles as though testing if I still belong to land or water.

They finally allow me to see Lira.

She lies beneath the shade of woven canopies built across the lagoon. She remains sleeping, her skin pale but her breath steady. The wise women tend to her with shells filled with pale blue salve and bowls of liquid that smell of roots and leaves. One of them tells me she took poison into her blood, barbs coated with the venom of river reeds. They say the Dumalog keep the antidote for their own, and they have given it to her freely.

"She will wake," says one of the women. "She's too angry to die."

That sounds like her.

I bow to the healers and move on.

Later, Oran brings me before the elders of Dumalog. There are five of them, seated beneath a canopy of whale bone and reed. They are old but unbent.

Oran introduces me, his hand resting on my shoulder. "Nogas, son of Rigo."

The name ripples through them like a wave breaking against rock.

One elder, skin dark as mountain stone, laughs quietly. "Rigo's boy? The tide does keep its promises."

Another leans forward. "Your father was a storm with legs. He could lift an oar thicker than my arm and laugh while the sea tried to drown him."

Oran nods. "He was the last to hold the tide at bay when Murong's armies came. He and Captain Tamdon fought until their spears broke. The sea took them both, but it gave us time."

I listen silently. I don't know how to wear their praise.

Oran leads me through the islands afterward. He shows me the children learning under the shade of palms, tracing letters in the sand.

"They will know the world," he says. "We teach them of rivers and kingdoms, so they remember what freedom costs."

A little boy runs up to me, handing me a small shell carved with the mark of a wave.

"For you, my lord," he says shyly. "My father says the tide never forgets who fights for it."

I close my hand over it. "Thank you."

Days pass quietly.

I train with the young men when my wounds allow it, sparring with spears, harpoons, and tridents. They fight with no fear, only rhythm, as though battle were a dance the sea taught them.

Then, one afternoon, Oran summons me to the shore.

My spear, shield, and belt lie waiting.

The shield gleams gold beneath the sun. Suba's gift. The spear hums when I lift it, as if it knows my heartbeat.

They ask me what I wish to do with my old clothing. The ones made in the colors of Tinigbasan.

"Destroy them," I answer. "That man died on the road, Shaman."

Oran studies me, and for the first time I see approval in his eyes. "Good. The sea cannot claim what still clings to the shore."

Later, I watch my Tinigbasan tunic and cloak burn in a firepit. I watch the ash and smoke rise into the wind.

That night, sleep does not come, so I walk the shore.

The horizon flickers with strange light, faint and gold, like the glimmer of a distant storm. The sea's breath grows uneasy.

Days later, I am called at dawn, to the council.

The elders are gathered beneath the same canopy, their faces grim.

Oran speaks first. "Our scouts report ships on the horizon. Dalidnon sails."

A pause.

"Envoys?" I ask.

"No," the shaman says. "The kingdoms do not send envoys to Dumalog. They send armies."

A man steps out of the shadows. He is tall, broad, and scarred, his hair bound with cord, his eyes like steely obsidian.

"I am Tamlak, Captain of the Dumalog navy. I'm the son of Tamdon, the man who died beside your father." He thumps his fist against his chest. "Chieftain Rigo was a giant in the waves. He saved my father's life twice before the third tide took them both. I have waited my whole life to see his blood rise again."

He pauses, then grins at me. "You will lead us, yes?"

I hesitate. "I have barely healed."

He laughs. "Then fight with your scars. The sea doesn't wait for the healed, only the willing."

Oran gestures to the sea. "Their ships approach fast. They have already dispatched canoes. It will not be long before they reach our shores."

Tamlak bares his teeth. "Then we'll meet them before they set foot."

The elders look to me.

"Your command, son of Rigo," says Oran. "Choose. The Dumalog will follow."

I can almost feel the weight of a title I never asked for pressing against my shoulders, anchoring me to the sand.

I turn to the horizon, watching blue bleeding into gray. The sails of Dalidnon glint like shark fins in the distance.

"We defend the isles," I say. "We hold the line. The sea is ours. Let's keep it that way."

The elders nod, murmuring among themselves.

Oran inclines his head gravely. "Then may the sea judge you worthy, as it did your father."

Tamlak springs into action, barking orders as he runs toward the waiting commanders. "Bring the call to arms! Sound the drums! Women and children to the inner islands, elders to the stone shelters!"

The beach erupts into motion. Shell horns wail. Warriors rush to their canoes, fastening blades to oars and nets to prows.

Oran turns to me, his hand heavy on my shoulder. "There is no turning back now."

I tighten my grip on my spear. "There never was."

Then I run with Tamlak, down the slope of sand, into the roar of the sea.

A tall wave crashes against the canoes as we push off. Spray hits my face, tasting like salt and fury. Ahead, the sails of Dalidnon draw closer with every heartbeat.

The drums of Dumalog thunder like a living heart.

And somewhere across the sea, I swear I feel another.

A heartbeat that answers mine.

CHAPTER 31

Spring of the Earth

ANINI

T HE WORLD EXPLODES INTO LIGHT.

The ground burns against my knees as I grab the fallen flower, clutching it to my chest.

I can't breathe.

Every sound folds into the roar of something ancient waking up.

Hands reach for me through the glare.

"Anini!" Sidlaw's voice, near and desperate.

"Anini!" my father shouts behind him.

Someone catches me. Strong arms. Steady heartbeat.

It's Sidlaw. I can smell the sea on him. I clutch at his sleeve without knowing why, gasping and trembling.

"Princess…"

But I am already pulling away.

The light hasn't left me. It's in my hands.

Burning. Trembling.

Alive.

The flower, the river-meets-the-sun bloom, blazes like a living star against my chest.

And then I hear her.

Kala's voice.

"When the time comes, decide with your whole heart…or be consumed by what you leave unchosen."

With your whole heart.

Decide.

Decide.

Decide.

The words echo, louder than Sidlaw calling, louder than my father's panicked shouts.

My feet move before my mind does.

The hall is behind me. The sound, the gasps, the confusion.

I'm running.

The wind tears through my hair.

The stone floors turn to grass, to earth, to the cliffside path.

The guards and handmaidens cry out behind me, but I don't stop.

I can't.

Every step is faster, freer, truer.

The air tastes like salt and the dew of sunrise.

The flower presses hot against my heart and the world seems to breathe with me.

He seems to breathe with me.

The clouds above begin to break.

Sunlight bursts through, flooding the path in gold.

The wind rises, catching my robes like sails.

I reach the edge.

Our cliff.

The same cliff where Nogas once stood between me and the sun. The same place where he gave me his cloak.

Our cliff.

And I think…

I have chosen.

"Anini!"

I can hear Sidlaw's voice behind me.

He's fast, faster than anyone I know, but not fast enough.

He grabs for me, and the light bursts outward.

A pulse.

A roar.

A wave of power that throws him backward as if the sky itself struck him.

He crashes to the ground with a cry, tumbling down the lower ridge.

More voices—guards, my father, maybe even the other rulers—shouting, rushing up the path.

But I can barely hear them.

Kala's voice fills my head again.

"Decide with your whole heart."

And I know what that means.

I clutch the flower tighter to my chest.

The heat sears my palms, but I don't let go.

"I want to remember," I say.

The wind stops.

The earth holds its breath.

"I want to remember how his heart beats."

My voice breaks.

"I want to remember how *mine* beats because of him."

And then…

The land answers.

It starts as a low groan beneath my feet, the sound of stone remembering it was once alive. The cliff shudders, cracks, splits open in a jagged line of light.

The ground collapses.

Not downward, but inward, as if folding around something buried deep. Rocks shatter, tumble, reform. The sea roars, pulled toward the cliffs, clawing at them with foaming fingers.

Then the world bursts open.

A geyser of light and water erupts, glowing gold and white, fire in liquid form. Steam pours into the air, warm and fragrant, not of salt but of flowers and rain.

The cliffside remakes itself before my eyes, breaking and reshaping, until the stone bleeds into a basin, a cradle of new rock holding a spring that blazes with molten blue.

Water gushes through cracks, spilling over edges, rushing toward the sea below.

The sound is like a thousand heartbeats colliding.

The air is heat and mist and radiance.

I'm standing at the edge of it, trembling, tears burning my cheeks.

Behind me, the world catches up.

Voices shout.

Feet pound.

Sidlaw, bruised and bleeding, scrambles up the path.

My father, the guards and maidens, the lords—they're all frozen in awe.

Sidlaw is the first to reach the edge. He looks at me as if I no longer made sense.

"What happened, Princess?" he calls out.

I laugh. Or maybe cry. I realize it's both. The tears are burning hot, like the water rising around me.

"The land remembers," I answer, my voice shaking. "The land remembers. It never forgot."

I lift the flower. It's still glowing, its light dancing over the new spring below.

"The flame met the stone," I say. "The river brought the sun."

And then the earth laughs.

A sound deeper than thunder, richer than song, rolling through the cliffs, through the sea, through my bones.

The surface of the spring explodes upward in a column of steam and light.

From it, Suba bursts forth.

Towering, dripping, radiant, laughter shaking the cliffs themselves. He slaps a hand against the earth, sending waves rolling outward.

"Princess, you called?"

My heart leaps. "Lord Suba…"

"My lady said you have need of a reminder," he booms, water cascading from his shoulders like silver rain. "And of course, I could *never* refuse my Princess of Steel."

The ground trembles beneath his grin.

I stand there, breathless and soaked, the flower still glowing against my chest.

I don't know what I've done.

I only know that the land has answered. That it heard me.

Somewhere beyond the horizon, I can feel him.

Nogas.

And I know.

The waves bear his name.

CHAPTER 32

Island of the Tide

Nogas

THE SKY BLEEDS RED.

War drums thunder through the mist.

The Dalidnon ships cut through the waves like blades through flesh.

Tamlak stands beside me on the prow of the war canoe, shouting orders over the roar of the wind. "Raise the nets! Hold the line! Wait for the turn of the tide!"

The Dumalog fleet fans out across the bay, a hundred boats made from wood and bone, indigo sails stitched with copper thread. The oars move in rhythm, chanting with every pull.

The sea answers us.

I stand at the front, spear in hand, golden shield glinting against the morning light.

Salt burns my wounds, but the pain only reminds me that I'm still alive.

"Ready, son of Rigo?" Tamlak grins, his teeth white against the spray.

"Always," I say.

He laughs. "Good. Then don't die before I do."

The Dalidnon ships are closer now, their sails gleaming bright blue with royal sigils. They are magnificent and terrible, bristling with archers and armored soldiers.

We are smaller, faster, fewer.

And we have nothing left to lose.

When the first arrows fly, they sound like rain.

We raise our shields.

Arrows snap against the golden sun.

One strikes my arm. I tear it free and throw it aside.

"Now!" Tamlak bellows.

The Dumalog canoes veer left and right, flanking the larger ships. Spears fly, grappling lines snap tight, warriors climb up the hulls.

The sea becomes chaos. A blur of bodies, foam, and smoke.

I leap onto the deck of the nearest Dalidnon ship, shield raised, spear spinning. The first soldier I strike falls before he can even scream. The next blocks my spear, but I ram my shield into his chest and hear ribs crack.

Blood slicks the deck.

Fire spreads from their oil pots.

The smell of iron fills the wind.

And still, I fight.

For her.

Then, suddenly, everything stops.

A ripple runs through the ocean, so deep it feels like the heartbeat of the world.

The current stills.

The wind falls silent.

Even the drums fade, one by one, until all that's left is the sound of breathing and the slow, shivering pulse beneath my feet.

The horizon begins to glow.

At first, I think it's fire. Perhaps the sun breaking wrong.

But then I see it.

Five rays of light.

Five, like the petals of her flower.

Five, like the sigil carved into my shield.

Five, the spokes of Suba's sun.

They shoot outward from the land, lancing across the water.

Gold, white, blue, crimson, and silver.

They slice through the mist, blood, and foam around us.

Each ray strikes something.

One touches the sea, turning the waves molten gold.

One hits my shield, and the whole world flares.

Another runs up the sail of the Dalidnon ship before me, igniting it in light.

The other pierces the clouds, tearing them open.

And the last, the brightest, sinks deep into the ocean's heart.

When it does, the sea moves.

Not like waves.

But a living thing remembering its shape.

The water draws inward, spiraling around the place the light entered. Foam collapses, spinning downward into a perfect circle.

The surface churns, hissing. Not from heat, but from birth.

And then the sea rises.

Stone bursts through the surface, black and shining like obsidian freshly forged.

Steam bellows from the cracks. Water pours down the newborn cliffs, roaring like rivers come to life.

An island, vast and radiant, heaves itself from the deep.

Every Dalidnon ship is tossed backward. Warriors scream. Sails tear.

The Dumalog canoes spin, caught in the upheaval, but none capsize. It's as if the sea spares us, knows us as its own.

I drop to one knee, shield still raised, the rays still dancing across its face. The gold glows hotter, almost unbearably so.

My reflection disappears from the surface.

Instead, I see Anini.

She's standing at the edge of the world, hair flying, the flower blazing against her heart.

Then I hear her voice, rolling through me like the tide.

Let the waves bear your name.

And the waves obey.

The island's rivers surge toward the sea, carving paths in molten rock. The spray burns my skin, but I can't look away.

The ocean isn't destroying.

It's remaking.

Tamlak grips the gunwale beside me. "By the bones of the depths…what sorcery is this?"

"Not sorcery," I say, voice shaking. "It's her."

The sea trembles again, and this time the light condenses into a spiral above the new island, a storm made of silk and fire, dark at its heart but shining at its edges.

From that whirling column, a voice rolls out like lightning from the depths.

"The river brought the sun."

The whirlpool bursts open.

And she rises.

Lady Kala's hair streams behind her like black water. Her gown is made of the sea itself, dark blue shot with stars and foam. She spins once, the air bending around her, waves bowing in her wake.

"Princess," she calls, the sound hitting every heart on every ship. *"You have remembered. You have chosen. The land answered, and the sea followed."*

She turns her gaze to me.

"Warrior of the Sun, Son of Rigo. The waves bear your name now. Your life will no longer be your own."

I try to speak, but the words vanish in the wind.

All I can do is watch as the storm around her builds, a beautiful shadow of a hurricane swirling over the island.

Tamlak drops his harpoon, falling to one knee in awe.

Even the Dalidnon ships stop their assault.

Men stare, mouths open, their weapons useless before such divinity.

Kala spreads her arms. *"The Rite of Shaping Sea is fulfilled. The flame has met the stone. The river has brought the sun. The world remembers its promise."*

The light brightens, reflecting in the five rays still etched on my shield. They pulse once, twice, five times, in perfect rhythm with my heartbeat.

And then, as quickly as it came, the brilliance softens.

The whirlwind settles. The island gleams, steaming gently in the sunlight.

Kala hovers above it, smiling faintly.

"The sea remembers," she says, softer now. "It always remembers those who love without fear."

Her gaze meets mine, and for a moment, I think I see Anini's reflection in her eyes.

Radiant and alive. Still unbroken.

Then Kala vanishes in a swirl of mist and water.

The ocean calms.

The Dumalog fleet is silent. The Dalidnon ships drift aimlessly. Every warrior on both sides lowers his weapon.

No one speaks.

Only the sea moves, breathing steadily.

I bow my head, pressing a bloodied hand to the sun carved into my shield. The rays are still warm. Five lines of gold, each pulsing faintly like veins.

"She's alive," I say.

Tamlak looks at me, voice trembling when he asks, "What now, Chieftain?"

I raise my head.

The island stands before me, newborn and glistening, where there was once only endless blue.

"We go to her."

CHAPTER 33

Anini

T HE SPRING STILL HISSES AND GLOWS AROUND ME, gold steam curling from the cracks in the earth.

Suba stands in the middle of it all, water cascading from his shoulders, laughter shaking the stones. He looks like he belongs to another age, one older than the mountains and the tides.

"In order for a new world to rise," he says, "the old one must first be destroyed. *Sira-an*, Princess of Steel. Destroy, so that something new can be forged."

I can't move. My hands are trembling.

In my palms, the river-meets-the-sun flower still glows faintly, five soft rays pulsing like heartbeats.

Then, as I watch, the light fades. The petals blacken at the edges, crumble, and scatter.

"Wait! No—" I try to catch them, but the dust slips through my fingers.

Suba only chuckles. "That's exactly what you did, Princess of Steel. You broke the world open."

The dust lands on the wet ground.

And from it, life springs forth.

Thick roots break through the soaked earth, twisting upward as if the island itself is taking a breath. Dark trunks rise, their bark steaming in the heat. Branches unfurl from the swelling ground, stretching toward the sky. And then, bursting through the brown-green stems, come the flowers. Clusters upon clusters of white-and-gold blooms, all at once spilling light and fragrance into the air like the island's first prayer.

"See?" Suba gestures proudly. "*River-meets-the-sun.* They grow here now, for the first time beyond the veil. Blessed by light, born of your boon."

"My boon?" My voice cracks. "I asked for nothing from your lady."

Suba tilts his head, looking like someone who knows too much. "Perhaps you didn't. Or perhaps what you asked for was too heavy for your lips to say. But your heart…Oh, Princess, your heart spoke. And Lady Kala heard it loudest of all."

Before I can answer, another voice shouts my name.

"Anini!"

Sidlaw stumbles into view, bruised and wild-eyed. He pushes in front of me, blade half-drawn.

"Stay behind me, Princess!" he snarls, squaring up to Suba. "What brings you to our shores, creature?"

Suba blinks, then looks genuinely confused. "Our shores? Little fish, the sea is older than any of your so-called kingdoms."

Sidlaw tightens his stance, but before he can make a move to strike, Suba leans down until their eyes meet.

"You were not asked to speak by the princess, were you, small fry?" says the giant, grinning. "This is between her and me."

"Enough!" comes my father's voice.

Datu Oyong arrives with guards and stewards, his robes soaked, his face ashen. "What are you doing here, Lord Suba?"

Suba straightens, towering over everyone. "Ah, the river-king himself. And what a delicate current you have made of your line."

"Answer me!" Oyong shouts, the air trembling with his fury.

Suba's grin fades. His eyes burn white.

The ground hums as though bracing itself.

When the giant speaks again, his voice shakes the sky. "SILENCE!"

The sound hammers through my bones. Everyone else drops to their knees, even my father.

"I speak for Lady Kala of the Pearl Waters as her consort," Suba thunders. "My lady owed your Princess of Steel a boon in the name of her mother, Rumina. I was sent to grant it, to make sure the flame met the stone of your peaks, so your land would remember it was never without the sea. They must be as one."

Oyong turns to me, eyes wide. "You asked for this?"

"I did not," I say. "But my heart spoke for me. It needed the land to remember."

The ground trembles.

The flowers around the spring begin to glow again, five bright rays from each bloom, shooting upward into the clouds.

Then, as if the sky itself breathes out, those rays explode outward—up, then down—striking the sea.

The world convulses.

The cliffs shake. The earth splits. The sound is so deep it feels like it's tearing through my chest.

Suba squints toward the horizon. "Ah. There she goes. And they call *me* dramatic."

Everyone looks to the sea.

And the light…

It's blinding.

Five rays, mirrored exactly in the same pattern as my flower, now blazing across the water. It's now reflected in the clouds, in the shield of every soldier, in the eyes of the gods.

The sea boils.

Then it rises.

Black stone bursts upward, molten and screaming, wrapped in steam and sunlight.

The waves crash outward, turning into walls of fire and foam.

"An island," someone gasps.

An island *rises.*

I stumble back as the cliffs crack beneath my feet.

Sidlaw grabs me, pulls me close, shielding me with his

arm. The ground rolls like a living beast, throwing us both down.

"Hold on!" he shouts.

But the land tilts. The rocks slide.

The whole world seems to come apart.

Guards tumble into the surf.

People and beasts scream.

The sea eats the lower cliffs and spits them out as shards of light.

I hit the ground hard, dirt and salt in my mouth. I can't tell if I'm screaming or laughing. The heat from the springs blinds me.

A shadow falls across me.

Suba's smiling knowingly, his hair streaming like ink. "My lady was occupied elsewhere. She was better suited to fulfill this boon than I. So perhaps you could say…" He kneels, scooping me into his arms as if I weigh nothing. "…we switched duties."

"Boon?" I gasp. "Who asked it?"

His smiles softens. His voice rumbles low. "You already know."

I blink at him, heart hammering. I do know.

"Nogas."

Suba nods solemnly. "The sea-born king of the Dumalog. Nogas, son of Rigo."

The world shatters again.

The roar of the sea fades to a pulse. The heat becomes light.

I try to speak. To ask.

How? Where? When?

But everything blurs.

My limbs go heavy.

My heart is too loud.

Suba's voice is distant and gentle now. "Rest, Princess of Steel. You've earned it."

The last thing I see is the horizon burning gold, the newborn island still rising from the heart of the sea, crowned by a storm shaped like a woman's form.

Lady Kala, swirling above it, dark and radiant, a whirlwind breaking the clouds.

Then the tide takes me.

CHAPTER 34

Shaping of the Current

Nogas

THE SEA IS QUIET NOW.

The roar of the storm has gone, the wind swallowed by the echo of what just happened.

The birth of an island. The unmaking of war.

Where the Dalidnon ships once stood proud and glittering, there is now wreckage scattered across the water. The ones not torn apart by the rising land drift aimlessly, their sails burnt, their masts broken. The sea itself seems to mourn them.

Behind us, the Dumalog canoes rock gently, held by invisible hands. Lady Kala's winds move us back toward the islands.

No one rows.

No one speaks.

When we reach the shore, the warriors climb down one

by one, stunned, dripping seawater and awe. We regroup wordlessly, unsure what comes next. Some whisper that the gods have ended the war. Some whisper that the end of days has begun.

I stand on the sand, spear and shield in hand, watching the light still pulsing across the sea.

Part of me wonders if I have died, if this shore is the afterlife.

And then the wind changes.

The air hums like the pause before thunder.

The sea parts. From it, she rises once more.

The dark whirlwind follows Lady Kala ashore, a crown of black clouds laced with lightning, a whirlpool made flesh. Her eyes are silver in the sun. Every drop of water seems to bow as she steps onto the sand.

All around me, the Dumalog drop to their knees, foreheads pressed to the earth.

Even Tamlak kneels without hesitation.

Oran walks forward, robes trailing in the wet sand, and falls to his knees before her.

Kala looks down at him, faintly amused. "Killing Agdan was a bold move, Shaman."

He lowers his head. "If my actions displease you, great lady, you may strike me down now."

Kala's voice is calm, rippling like low tide. "Your mortal affairs are not ours to judge. We honored Agdan at the end. We will do the same for you when your time comes."

"Then I thank you, for mercy and memory," says Oran. "I never did thank you for saving my blood."

Kala's eyes soften. "That child was more mine than yours,

Oran. It was my honor to see Rumina grow. My only regret is that she did not live long enough to see her child change the world."

Oran closes his eyes. "I know of what you speak, great lady. And I will see her in the seas beyond ours soon, I am certain."

Kala inclines her head. "Then may that reunion come with peace, not sorrow."

Then her gaze moves to me.

"Mountain warrior," she says, and the air itself bends around her words. Then, with a smile, she adds, "Or shall I say…Sea-King?"

I drop to one knee before her. "Nogas, great lady."

She sighs, rolling her eyes slightly, half-amused. "You are exactly like Suba. No affectations. Where he smiles, you brood. But the same kind of pure heart lies underneath. I can't say I blame Anini."

My head jerks up. "Forgive me?"

Kala's smile turns knowing. "Nothing to forgive, boy. Your boon is complete."

She gestures toward my shield.

It begins to glow.

Five rays of light pulse from its center. Gold, red, silver, white, and blue; the same colors that tore through the sky. They burn brighter, then dim, the gold deepening into a richer and darker hue, like the sun setting into the sea.

"I did not ask for any boon, great lady," I say. "I wanted nothing."

"You did," Kala answers. "We heard it from across the

veil, Sea-King. You were fighting for her. For her will, her choice. That was your boon. *Her choice.*"

She takes a step closer. "And across the waters, she didn't want to forget you. So I gave her something that would make the world remember you. Always."

Her hand sweeps toward the horizon, where the newborn island still smolders in gold and smoke.

"The island. In your name. The Princess of Tinigbasan never wanted you forgotten. Now the world will always speak your name in wonder and awe."

For a moment, I cannot breathe.

I stare at the island.

At *Nogas Island*, though I do not yet dare call it that.

My throat burns. My chest aches.

I realize too late that my face is wet.

I am crying.

Kala's voice softens, warm as dawn. "You gave her choice. And she chose you. She chose to remember you. She chose for the water to bear your name. And now it does."

She steps closer, pressing her palm gently to my forehead. "The Rite of Shaping Sea is complete. The name *Nogas* shall live in the whispers of the waves for all eternity."

A warmth floods through me. My shield hums. The sand glows beneath my knees.

"Now rise," she commands. "Bring these people to their rightful kingdom. To your land."

She turns toward the sea and raises her hand.

The waters part once more.

Stone rises from the depths. They form massive,

glistening steps that stretch across the strait from the Dumalog isles to the new island. The sea glows around them.

The people gasp, bowing low, weeping with awe.

Kala lowers her hand, her storm slowly calming. She glances toward Oran one last time and nods.

In answer, Oran lowers his head to the ground.

Then she looks at me once more, and smiles. "You will understand in time, Sea-King. Love is the oldest current of all."

With that, she vanishes, dissolving into mist and shadow.

Silence follows. Only the sea breathes.

I stand, turning to the people who kneel before me.

My people, though I still cannot believe it.

But something tugs at me, deep and tight, pulling me toward the mainland.

Toward her.

Suddenly, my chest tightens.

My wounds burn again, the old pain roaring back to life.

And I feel her name in my blood.

"Anini," I whisper to the tides.

The world lurches.

The light fades.

And I fall.

CHAPTER 35

Rite of Kings

Anini

When I open my eyes, the world sways like the sea.

The ceiling above me blurs, bamboo and woven leaves, dimly gold under filtered light.

My throat is dry. My limbs are heavy.

Every breath feels strange and new, as if I'd forgotten how.

And then, through the haze, I see Sidlaw.

He's sitting beside my mats, his hair dishevelled. His tunic looks rumpled. His eyes are ringed in gray, the tiredness carved into his face like stone worn by the tide. There's a sheen of salt on his skin, as if he's been living in the wind too long.

"You're awake," he says softly.

"Sidlaw…" I try to speak, but my throat cracks. "How long…?"

"Five days."

Five.

The number lands like a weight in my chest.

He leans forward, pours water into a clay cup, and steadies it against my lips. His hands shake. I drink, the water cool and strange, the taste of earth in every drop.

"You wouldn't wake," he murmurs. "Not even when the healers burned incense, or called your name. You just…kept whispering his."

The silence after cuts like a blade.

Sidlaw looks down, shoulders tense, his voice low. "You don't have to talk about it now. I didn't want to… burden you."

"What happened?" I ask. "The last thing I remember was…the cliff."

He breathes out slowly, as though holding too much air for too long. "You wouldn't stop running. The world split open and the sea itself climbed the sky. It's been chaos since then."

His tone changes, now more restrained. "Dalidnon's eastern fleet…it's gone. Datu Radul sent it against the Dumalog. Not one ship returned whole."

I try to sit up, but the dizziness hits hard. "Gone?"

"Yes." He looks away, jaw tight. "The Dumalog now have their own kingdom. The island, and all the smaller ones around it. A fortress of coral and molten stone. It's only a matter of time before they advance toward the mainland. Their fleets sail under new banners."

I stare at him, my heart pounding. "Whose banners?"

He hesitates. "Their armies are led by a captain named Tamlak. I know him from battles before. He's fierce, ruthless, cunning. But their chief…"

He swallows hard. "Their chieftain is the son of Rigo. The sea-born king of the Dumalog. They call him Nogas."

The sound of his name rips through me.

For a heartbeat, I can't speak.

The air vanishes from the room.

Nogas.

Every memory rushes back like water.

The light. The spring. The island rising.

Suba's echoing laughter.

"You already know."

My body trembles. I can feel it again. The surge of heat from the flower, the rays of gold splitting the sky, the pulse of his name in my veins.

I hear myself whisper, "Suba said it. The sea-born king of the Dumalog. Nogas, son of Rigo. Is this really true?"

Sidlaw's silence is answer enough.

"Perhaps," he says finally, "it's better if you hear the rest from someone who knows more than I."

He stands, smoothing his sleeves as if to compose himself.

"I'll send them in," he tells me quietly.

"Wait." My voice catches. "Sidlaw, what happens now?"

He stops by the doorway, shoulders hunched as if he carries the weight of the fallen ships.

"These past days," he says, "the rulers have been

too busy fighting a real war to talk of anything else. The Dumalog have proven themselves real. They have their king, their land. The giant and the mermaid queen made it all real, Princess. And sometimes what is real and what is spoken of are as different as death and living."

Then he bows, low and weary.

"Rest, Princess," he says. "You'll need your strength for what's coming."

Sidlaw leaves before I can call him back.

The room feels colder without him. The silence is thick enough to choke on.

"Princess?"

The voice is soft, trembling, achingly familiar.

I look up.

And everything in me breaks.

"Lira!"

She's standing in the doorway, wrapped in linen and sunlight. Her right arm is bandaged to the elbow, her hair unbound, her eyes wet and shining. For a moment we just stare at each other.

Then I'm out of my mats and blankets, unsteady, falling into her arms.

"Lira! Oh, gods! You're alive…"

She lets out a choked sob, clutching me tight. "My Princess. My light. I thought I'd never see you again."

We both start crying. Ugly, gasping, human tears. I hold her face, brush the salt from her cheeks. She smells like herbs and the sea.

"I thought you were dead," I say.

"I almost was." Her voice shakes. "We both were."

She pulls back slightly, brushing hair from my face, her eyes red. "After the ambush, after Sidlaw carried you away…Nogas and I were still fighting. He refused to fall. He took arrows and blades, but he kept going. When the raiders surrounded us, he stood like the gods had carved him from fire. He said your name with every breath."

I close my eyes.

"And then?" I ask, forcing the words past the lump in my throat.

"Then the Dumalog and Kalisidlan…stopped." Her tone softens. "They weren't raiders. They were warriors. Their shaman, Oran, stopped the fight. They carried us both to their isles. They didn't kill us. They treated our wounds, fed us, and healed us."

Her voice cracks again. "Nogas was nearly gone, Princess. They said his blood had run too deep. But their shaman knew something. He kept saying, *'The sea doesn't drown its own.'* And then…they called him their king."

"King," I echo, still in disbelief.

Lira hesitates. "The chief of them all. He is the son of Rigo. The last chief of Dumalog, the one who fell when Datu Murong's armies once burned the isles. The Dumalog say their bloodline has returned. That the sea crowned him. That the gods themselves named him ruler."

I grip her hands tighter. "And what about you?"

"Their wise women healed me. And when I could walk, their shaman Oran sent me back, along with the Tinigbasan handmaidens and guards—as envoy."

"Envoy?"

She nods. "An envoy bearing the chieftain's challenge. His message to the lords of Hamtic."

I swallow. "What message?"

She looks down, her voice trembling. "The Rite of Binding Blood. He calls upon the lords of Hamtic to choose a champion to face him."

The words echo through me. "The Rite. He's invoking the old laws. The same way he did with Suba."

"Yes."

"And if he wins?"

"If he wins," Lira says, "the islands and the coast—all of Hamtic—will belong to him."

The weight of it crushes the breath from my lungs.

I stumble back, shaking my head. "Why? Why would he…?"

Her eyes are glassy with tears. "I think he believes he must. For his people. For the sea. For you."

I cover my mouth, trying to keep from breaking again. "He can't. He can't do this."

But Lira doesn't answer.

Her silence is worse than any truth.

Finally, she takes a deep, shuddering breath. "There's more."

I know from her eyes that I won't like what she's about to say.

"The lords of Hamtic have already chosen their champion."

My heart lurches. "Who?"

Lira hesitates. Then, she answers softly.

"Sidlaw."

The world seems to stop.
I feel it in my bones then.
That same light, that same burning.
But this time it's not divine.
It's heartbreak.
And everything goes still.

CHAPTER 36

Nogas

S EVEN DAYS.

Seven days since the island rose from the deep and everything I thought I knew broke open with it.

In seven days, the world has changed.

Where there was once nothing but scattered islets and huts, now stands a living kingdom. Smoke rises from new hearths built on sand. Children laugh near the springs that steam at dawn. Fishers carve new boats from the driftwood the sea delivers every morning, saying the water gives what it owes.

The Dumalog have begun to move their families here, guided by Oran, the scholars, and the wise women. Every day, another canoe arrives from the outer isles—people of the reefs, coral-hunters, boat dwellers, refugees from kingdoms that once claimed their coasts. They come worn yet hopeful, clutching nets, relics, and stories.

Just like my father did when he lived, I offered shelter to all who needed it.

They call this place *Isla Sang Kabuhi*.

The Island of Life.

Oran says it's the gods' sign that the sea remembers.

To me, it feels heavier than that. It feels as if the sea remembers too much.

By the time the sun breaks the horizon, I'm already standing on the beach, spear in hand, gold shield strapped to my back. The surf crashes around my ankles. Its rhythm sounds like a heartbeat that never stops.

Tamlak waits nearby, giving quiet orders to his captains as the Dumalog navy lines the shore. They look like an army born of tide and thunder, their canoes carved with teeth of bone and spines of coral, sails dyed the color of Lady Kala's dark storm.

Oran stands beside me, robes drawn close, his eyes on the sea. His voice is low, like a memory.

"They accepted the challenge."

"Yes," I answer. "The Rite of Binding Blood."

He nods gravely. "So the kingdoms have agreed to meet you at Tinigbasan's river grounds. Fitting, don't you think? Where water and land once met to forge their pacts, the sea now returns to claim its due."

I glance at him. "You've wanted this a long time, haven't you?"

"I've wanted balance," he says. "Saraya saw what would come. She saw Hamtic's greed, their endless grasping. The sea took her, but her words still live. You will fulfill what she died for. And perhaps…my blood will see the world she dreamed of."

His blood.

Anini.

I turn away before the ache in my chest can show.

Tamlak strides toward us. He stops before me, his weathered face creased but steady. "The men are ready, Chieftain. The canoes are armed, but we'll keep them behind the veil of reefs until your word."

"You're not coming," I remind him.

"No." His tone is firm. "The island must be guarded. The gods gifted it through you, Son of Rigo. I will not see it fall while you stand in another man's court. Oran goes with you. I stay to protect what you have built."

"What we have built, Captain," I correct him.

Tamlak smiles faintly, nodding. "Then I shall protect what is *ours.*"

Before I can speak again, a movement at the far end of the beach catches my eye.

Figures, tall and cloaked, walking down the slope of rock.

One strides ahead of the rest, his gait familiar even against the glare of the sun.

Bantawan.

The men behind him bear the sigils of Kalisidlan, flame and mountain, their colors burnt red and black.

The mountain tribes.

My tribe, a lifetime ago.

He looks older, wearier, but still carries himself like the stone he came from.

When he reaches me, he stops a few paces away. For a heartbeat, neither of us speaks. The sea fills the silence between us.

"I didn't think you'd come, Chieftain," I say at last.

"I didn't think I'd have to," he answers. "But the world has a way of forcing old men to finish what they began."

"You knew," I say quietly. "But you never told me."

He breathes out, slow and heavy. "The boy who could not be broken by pain. Only one line bred that kind of fire. Chieftain Rigo's."

I look away, my throat tightening. "You could have told me. All of my life, I believed I had no blood."

"I could have," he agrees. "But you were not ready. You had to grow among the stone first. To understand what weight feels like before you could bear the sea. Had I told you, you would have drowned in your own name."

There's a long pause.

"Why now?" I ask. "Why stand with me now?"

He takes a step closer, eyes unwavering. "Because you did what no king of Hamtic has done in generations. You rose. You forged land from the sea. You made the gods remember their promises. The mountain tribes have seen it. The Kalisidlan remember you as their own. And now they will fight beside you, with the Dumalog."

I stare at him. "You mean…"

He nods. "The allegiance of Kalisidlan is yours. The mountain tribes and the forest clans. All of them, Nogas. I bring you their oath."

The wind catches the edges of his cloak, revealing the burn marks across his arms, the marks of brotherhood and loyalty carved into his flesh.

My throat tightens at the sight.

"Why?" The question leaves my lips before I can hold it back.

"Because it's time," Bantawan says. "Time for the kingdoms to remember the blood they tried to bury. You carry both the sea and the mountain. The water and the stone. You are the storm that ends their rule."

He drops to one knee before me, head bowed, fist pressed against his chest. All the men behind him drop to their knees, pressing their foreheads to the sand.

The sight hits me like waves.

I bow my head, forcing out breath. "You shouldn't kneel."

"Then let me stand as your ally," he says, voice breaking. "But know this, Nogas. To me, you will always be the boy I raised as my own."

Something inside me breaks.

I reach for him, grip his arm, pull him up. "Then rise, Bantawan. Rise as an ally. But never forget, you are still the father fate chose for me."

He meets my eyes, and for a long moment, we don't speak. We don't have to.

Behind him, the warriors of Kalisidlan keep their heads and eyes lowered as they rise, their own spears glinting in the sun.

I turn to Tamlak and Oran, to the gathered elders, the captains, the women and children watching from the dunes.

"My people," I say, my voice rising over the surf, "we have

built this land from nothing but blood and memory. Guard it well. Protect it. Whatever comes from the kingdoms, stand your ground. This island is ours now. No tide will wash it away, as long as a Dumalog breathes."

They kneel as one, heads bowed to the sand.

Then the chant begins.

Low at first, then rising, a tide of voices rolling across the beach.

"Nogas. Anak sang Kadagatan. Anak sang Kabuhi. Hari sang Dumalog."

Son of the Sea. Son of Life. King of the Dumalog.

The chant follows us as we walk toward the waiting war canoe, carved with the faces of sharks and suns.

Tamlak grips my shoulder before I step in.

"When you return," he says, "you'll return as more than our chief."

"Or less," I say quietly.

He smiles faintly. "If the sea wills it, you will still rise."

I nod, unable to trust my voice.

Oran steps in beside me, robes sweeping across the hull. "The tide awaits."

The warriors push us out. The canoe catches the current. Hundreds more follow, bearing leaders and warriors of the sea tribes.

The island grows smaller behind us, a dark crown in the gold morning light.

The chant fades into the wind, carried away by the waves until it sounds like something older than time.

And as the shore disappears, I lift my gaze to the direction of Tinigbasan.

The direction of her.

My hands tighten on the spear.

Anini.

Every wave that carries me forward feels like a heartbeat that belongs to her.

I whisper to the wind, "Let the gods bear witness. The blood I spill will not be for conquest. It will be for choice."

The sea answers with a roar.

Then we sail toward the battle that will change the fate of all.

CHAPTER 37

Anini

THE LIGHT DIES SLOWLY TODAY.

My library smells of salt and ink, of wind slipping through bamboo slats and pages that have tasted too much of the world. The roof creaks softly, like an old friend breathing.

From the window, I can see the line of guards patrolling the sand. Beyond them, the sea holds its breath. Hundreds of Dumalog canoes lie still across the water, their dark sails whipping in the breeze.

Tomorrow, the Rite of Binding Blood will take place.

Tomorrow, the gods will decide who owns the kingdoms and the sea.

I run my fingers across the edge of a scroll and say to no one, "Do we really own any of it, at all?"

The answer is a wave, folding itself against the shore.

Then footsteps rise from the stone paths. I recognize Mion's careful, deliberate tread.

"Princess."

He bows low at the entrance, his shadow stretching across the woven mats. Lira follows behind him, pale in the slant of sunset.

"The shaman of Dumalog requests an audience," Mion says. "Your father has given permission, on condition that I and Lady Lira accompany you, and that their weapons remain outside. They bring tokens. Scrolls, inspected and found harmless. The shaman says he has heard of your collection."

"Then let him see it," I say, rising to my feet. "And let him see that Tinigbasan is not afraid of words."

Mion nods once, then leaves to give the order.

Lira joins me, then we wait. The wind hums low against the roof.

Then the door opens.

The first to enter is tall and robed in deep indigo, his hair dark silver and bound at his nape. I know right away it's the shaman. His face bears the stillness of one who has seen too much and yet learned how to survive it. Behind him walks a scholar, hooded and taller, carrying a bundle of scrolls tied with white cord.

They bow, the torchlight trembling on their robes.

"Princess Anini of Tinigbasan," Mion announces. "Shaman Oran of Dumalog, and his attendant."

"Welcome," I say. "You honor me."

"The honor is mine," Oran replies, voice like wind through coral. "I have come bearing words, Princess, not weapons. I thought it only right that a keeper of scrolls should receive them."

"Words can wound sharper than weapons, Shaman," I say lightly.

His mouth tilts, a ghost of a smile. "Then let us pray these heal instead."

He gestures for his attendant to step forward. The figure sets the scrolls gently upon the table before me.

Something about the curve of those hands stops my breath.

The scholar straightens.

Then the hood falls.

And my world ends.

"Nogas."

His name leaves me before I can stop it, torn from somewhere between prayer and disbelief.

Lira gasps.

Mion goes still.

Even the sea seems to pause against the cliffs.

Nogas looks at me with those eyes that hold the storms I've been running from, and every part of me remembers it all.

The taste of rain on his lips. The warmth of blood on his hands.

The way he said, *I will destroy every lie for you.*

Before I can move, he does.

One step, then two.

And his mouth is on mine.

I don't think, don't breathe, don't care.

He kisses me like the world never ended, like every god watching us would have to close their eyes.

It is fever and memory.

It is the sound of waves breaking through me.

I forget Lira. I forget Mion.

I forget the war and the Rite and the kingdoms.

I remember only us.

When Nogas pulls away, I'm trembling, halfway broken, halfway alive.

"I thought you died," I say shakily.

"I did," he answers softly, tracing my cheeks with his fingers, his eyes never leaving mine. "And yet I came back. The sea was not done with me."

Behind him, Oran clears his throat, a quiet, understanding sound.

"Forgive me, Princess. It seems my scrolls carry more than words."

Nogas turns slightly toward him, and I see it.

Respect, the kind a warrior gives a father he never had.

"Princess," he says, "this is Shaman Oran, the one who found me after the battle."

Oran inclines his head. "And perhaps the one you should have met long before. For I am not only shaman of Dumalog."

His eyes look distant with memory as he continues. "I was once of Tinigbasan. I was the lover of Saraya, the oracle condemned by your ancestors. She prophesied that the river would meet the sun, and that the blood of the sea would rise to reclaim the land."

Lira grips my arm. "The stories of the elders…are true, then? The prophecy of the river and the sun?"

Oran pauses to look between me and Lira. "Together, they will change the world. That's what Saraya told Datu Murong back then, but he ordered her executed. We both escaped the kingdom. We had a daughter, Rumina."

The room blurs. I stumble backward, but Lira holds me steady.

"Saraya's life is in the scrolls I bring you now, Princess," he says quietly. "Her story. And mine."

"You…you're my grandfather," I manage.

His gaze gentles, old sorrow folding around it. "By blood, yes. By spirit, perhaps not. I lost both Saraya and Rumina to the sea. The same sea that now calls you back."

A tremor builds in my chest. "Why come now? Why reveal yourself only at the brink of war?"

"Because this is not merely a war of men," Oran says. "It is the closing of one age and the birth of another. The gods will choose whose blood shapes the next dawn. And it must be witnessed by all who remember how it began."

He steps closer, and his voice drops. "Your mother's blood was both river and the sea. Yours is the same. And in that, child, lies the weight of prophecy. The prophecy she died for. The one that made Tinigbasan hunt her."

I look at Nogas, his face shadowed.

"And now we live them," I say.

His jaw tightens. "If living means bleeding for them, then yes."

Silence.

The sound of the tide presses against the walls like breath.

Then Nogas turns to Mion, bowing low. "Captain Mion, I owe you an apology. I failed in my oath. I left her unguarded."

Mion studies him quietly, then says, "You died protecting her. That is more than most men ever do. Your next life is your own, boy. Spend it as you will."

Nogas' throat works, and I see his shoulders tighten. "Then may the gods forgive me for what I will spend it on."

Lira wipes her eyes. "Nogas…"

He turns to her, and his voice softens. "Thank you, Lady Lira, for standing with me in battle."

She shakes her head. "You brought my princess to life."

Then his gaze returns to me. It says everything.

Gratitude. Grief. Love. All tangled.

And I can't bear it.

I step closer again until I can feel his heat, his breath.

"You don't have to fight," I say. "Please. They can have their kingdoms. We can run. We can live."

Nogas shakes his head, smiling the way men do when they have already accepted their fate. "And where would we run, Princess? The sea is not wide enough to hide us. Your duties will call you back. My people will call me forward. We are made of duty, not escape."

"I don't care," I say, my voice breaking. "I love you. Do you hear me? I love you."

His eyes close. A tear slips down his cheek before he can stop it.

"And I will love you, Anini," he says, "until the gods forget my name."

My heart shatters at the words. I reach for him, but he steps back.

"I have to go," he says. "The Rite begins at dawn. If I die, let it be for something that will give you choice, not chains."

"Nogas, please…"

He takes my hand, presses it to his heart. "Remember me when the waves touch the cliffs. That's where I will be."

I can't stop my own tears now. They fall fast, hot, unstoppable.

"Please, Nogas. Please don't leave me again."

He smiles. It's the kind of smile that destroys.

"If I could choose, I never would. You know that."

Then he releases my hand.

Oran bows to me once more. "Princess, I wrote all these scrolls myself. They tell the story of your grandmother, and the life of Chieftain Rigo of the Dumalog. Read them. May Saraya's truth live in her blood. May Rigo's story never carry falsehood again, not after everything he has died for and what his son fights for now."

Then he turns to Nogas and Mion, nodding. Together they walk toward the door.

But before they cross the threshold, I run.

One last time.

"NOGAS!"

He turns, startled.

I throw my arms around him, burying my face in his chest.

"Stop fighting," I choke out. "We don't need to win. We just need to live."

He holds me tight, for a heartbeat, maybe two. Then he pulls back, cupping my face in his hands.

"Then live, my love," he says softly. "Live enough for both of us."

"Don't say that…" I breathe, but the words melt away.

He presses his forehead to mine, his arms going around me.

"I will find you again, Anini. Even if it's in another life. Let this be my vow to you."

And then he kisses me.

Just once. Trembling.

And final.

When he lets go, I fall.

Lira catches me as the door closes behind him.

Outside, the sea crashes against the cliffs.

It sounds like a promise breaking.

The hall is too loud.

Laughter spills like wine, thick and clouded. Servants bring in roasted fish, fresh fruit, and baskets of steaming rice. Every cup is raised to Sidlaw, the champion of Hamtic, the one who will fight for our honor at dawn.

But underneath it all, the air is heavy.

Each smile too forced. Every cheer too quick.

No one dares to say it aloud, but we all feel it.

This could be our last feast before something breaks forever.

My father drinks deeply from his cup and calls Sidlaw *the pillar of the kingdom, the blade of Hamtic, the son of its thunder.* The lords echo him, all applause and clatter.

Sidlaw laughs when they call his name, but the sound doesn't reach his eyes.

I can feel him glance toward me sometimes, across the long table lined with trays of food and jugs of wine.

I don't return his gaze. I can't.

By the time the feast ends, the moon has climbed high. My father retires first, his voice thick from drink, his shoulders bowed under the weight of everything unsaid. One by one, the lords follow, their laughter fading down the corridors until only a few guards remain.

Then Sidlaw turns to me.

"Princess," he says quietly. "May I escort you back to your palace?"

I nod. "Of course."

Four of the royal guards fall into step behind us. We walk through the long passage that leads toward the shore, the sound of the sea growing louder with every step.

The path is lined with torches, their flames bending in the wind. Somewhere beyond the cliffs, I can hear the waves hammering against stone, like a heartbeat that won't slow.

For a while, neither of us speaks. Then I say softly, "Tell me about your travels."

Sidlaw glances at me. "My travels?"

"Yes. You have seen more of the world than I ever will. Tell me what it was like. Growing up, sailing, fighting. How much of the world have you seen?"

A smile ghosts across his lips. "Too much, perhaps. And not enough."

I look up at him. "Please."

So he tells me.

"I left Dalidnon when I was fourteen," he says. "My father sent me to learn with the trade fleet. To see the lands beyond our own. I thought it was exile then, punishment for my arrogance. But it was the best thing that could have happened to me."

He pauses, watching the torchlight tremble on the sand. "I've seen the markets of Surig, where gold is traded like grain. I've seen the ruins of Nagsara, where temples crumble into the sea. I've witnessed masters of the rarest metals forge indestructible weapons. I've sailed through storms that split the sky, and I've seen men die clinging to ropes that tied them to their ships. I learned early in my travels that the sea takes what it wants."

His voice softens. "And I learned that kingdoms, no matter how grand, are only as good as those who rule them. Power means nothing if those who wield it don't listen, or learn, or care. I used to believe strength was everything. That being loud, fierce, unyielding would make me worthy of my name. But I was wrong."

He looks at me then, and for the first time, there's no prince in his eyes.

Only the man.

"I learned that strength is quiet. It's knowing when to bow, when to stand, when to walk away. It's understanding the people you're meant to protect, not just commanding them. That is why I watch, Princess. Why I listen. Because I have seen what happens when rulers don't."

"You've changed, Sidlaw," I tell him. "For the better, truth be told."

He smiles faintly. "You said once that I never would. I suppose I proved you wrong, didn't I?"

I smile back, though I know there is more sorrow than lightness in it.

We reach the front of my palace, the small outer hall where the sea can be heard through the woven walls. The guards stop a short distance away, their armor catching the moonlight.

Sidlaw stops by the doorway. "You should rest, Princess. Tomorrow will be long."

I nod, but I can't quite bring myself to step inside yet.

He hesitates, then says, "You know…that is what I've always admired about you."

I turn to him. "What is?"

"Your quiet," he says. "Not the silence of fear, but of thought. You listen. You learn. You see. You understand. Not just scrolls, not just words. People. That is what makes you different from all the nobles I've ever met."

He takes a slow breath, his eyes searching mine. "Perhaps that's why you hated me so much when we were children."

I stare at him. "Hated you?"

He laughs softly. "You must remember it. You were always serious, always learning, while I…" He shakes his head. "I was loud, proud, foolish. The kind of boy you couldn't stand to be near. The kind who thought bravery meant shouting the loudest."

I can't help it. I smile a little. "You were insufferable."

"I was," he admits. "Because I thought that's what made me seen. I wanted your attention. But every time I reached for it, your disdain burned hotter. So I tried harder, until I became the very thing you despised."

His voice grows quieter, a little raw at the edges. "It wasn't disdain that I saw in your eyes that frightened me, Anini. It was the truth. You saw through me. Saw exactly what I was. Unworthy."

"Sidlaw—"

He shakes his head. "Please let me finish. You don't know what it does to a man to be looked at by the one he admires most and know he will never be enough. I spent sun-cycles trying to change that."

"Why would you say that?"

"Because it's true," he says. "Because you were everything I wasn't. You're patient, wise, kind. And I…" He pauses, seemingly steadying himself. "I was a boy trying to impress a star."

"We were children, Sidlaw," I say, the words scraping my throat.

"Perhaps," he says. "But we're not anymore."

He takes a step closer, stopping just short of touching me. "I hope you will give me the chance to prove myself worthy of you. Not as a prince of Dalidnon, not as a warrior of Hamtic, but as a man. A man worthy of your gaze…and your respect."

He swallows. "Perhaps, someday, if the gods will it…a man worthy of your love."

My breath catches.

For a long moment, we just stand there, the waves whispering below the cliffs, as if they're holding their breath with us.

Then I finally speak, my voice trembling. "May the gods watch over you tomorrow, Sidlaw. And honor what you fight for."

He bows his head solemnly. "And may they keep you safe, Princess."

He steps back.

"Goodnight, Anini."

"Goodnight."

He turns away, his shadow stretching long in the torchlight as he walks down the path toward the Datu's grounds. Two of the guards follow in silence, their footsteps fading into the night. The other two take their posts at the entrance of my own palace.

I stay where I am, hands clenched. I don't move until they're gone. Until the sound of armor is swallowed by the wind.

Once I enter my hut, I sink to my knees, pressing my palm to the floor, my body trembling.

And I cry.

My empty hall fills with the sound of quiet, broken sobs that no one will ever hear.

Because tomorrow, men will fight in my name.

And I will have to watch.

CHAPTER 38

Dawn of Freedom

Nogas

The sea is restless with the dawn, tossing and turning in warning.

The sun is only a pale coin behind a veil of gray, its light stretching thin across the shore of Tinigbasan. The wind carries the sound of drums, steady like a heartbeat waiting to break.

I stand at the edge of the great fighting ground carved into the sand, a wide circle bordered by blackened stones. Beyond it rise the cliffs, where banners of the three kingdoms snap like wounded birds.

Tinigbasan. Dalidnon.

And Dumalog.

The people are everywhere.

Thousands of them, their faces solemn, expectant. Some stand in silence, others chant prayers to gods. The lords of

Hamtic are seated on their raised platform, watching. Their armor gleams, their hands rest on the hilts of their ceremonial blades.

Datu Oyong and Datu Radul sit at the center.

Anini sits next to her father, dressed in white and gold, her hair braided in silver cords, a flower pinned over her heart. It looks like the bloom once given by Suba, then blessed by Lady Kala. Her gaze is distant, her posture regal, but I can see the tightness in her jaw.

When she looks up, she sees me.

And the world stops moving.

Everything else—the wind, the currents, the crowd— falls away.

For a heartbeat, there is only her and me.

And in her eyes I see everything I have fought for.

And everything I will lose.

Oran stands beside me, his robe trailing over the sand. His voice is ancient in its calm.

"The gods are watching, boy. Not for who wins. For who endures."

"I know."

Across the circle, Sidlaw enters with the shaman of Dalidnon.

The prince wears only loose fighting trousers bound at the waist, his upper body bare. His skin gleams with oil, his muscles carved from cycles at sea and war.

The people of Dalidnon and the rest of the coast chant his name.

Sidlaw, son of the thunder, blade of Hamtic.

He meets my gaze across the sand.

I see no hate in his eyes, only a resigned understanding.

The shaman of Dalidnon, draped in white linen streaked with ash, raises his staff. The crowd stills. Even the sea seems to hold its breath.

"The Rite of Binding Blood," the shaman intones, his voice deep and resonant, carried by the wind. "A tradition older than kings, honored by gods and men. Here, no weapon is allowed but man himself. No bloodline is untouchable. Two men enter the circle, one by choice, one by challenge. Only death or surrender ends the rite."

He looks to me. "Do you, Nogas of Dumalog, son of Rigo, chosen by the sea, challenger of the lords of Hamtic, accept this rite in the eyes of gods and men?"

I bow my head. "I do."

He turns to Sidlaw. "And you, Sidlaw of Dalidnon, son of Radul, prince of the thunder, champion of Hamtic, do you accept this rite?"

Sidlaw straightens. "I do."

"Then let this ground be sacred," says the shaman. "Let blood be your witness. Let the gods remember what you were willing to die for."

He spreads his arms wide, and the crowd chants, low and rhythmic.

Dugo. Dugo. Dugo.

Blood. Blood. Blood.

Oran leans close to me. "You know what this means."

"Yes," I answer. "There is no turning back now."

The shaman steps back from the circle, leaving only the two of us within.

But before I face Sidlaw, I turn.

Toward Anini.

Every guard moves instantly, hands to their hilts. The lords rise, murmuring in confusion.

But I do not reach for a weapon.

I walk until I am close enough to see her tears glint in the morning light. Then I drop to my knees, lowering my head until my forehead touches the sand.

Gasps ripple through the crowd.

"Princess," I say, my voice breaking the silence. "This is where your freedom begins. Remember this moment. Whatever happens next…please remember it."

Her breath catches. I feel it like a wind against my soul.

When I lift my head, our eyes meet again.

It is as if we are alone in the world.

Her lips part, trembling.

Nogas…please.

But I can't answer her.

I stand, turning away, walking back to the center of the circle.

The air is charged. Sidlaw steps closer, each movement measured. The sand ripples under our feet, soft and unsteady.

He nods once. "Chieftain of Dumalog."

"Champion of Hamtic."

We circle each other, slowly, silently. The crowd watches, rapt.

Every sound is louder now. The rasp of sand beneath our feet. The hiss of the wind against the cliffs.

My muscles coil, every instinct screaming for patience. He is bigger, but slower. Stronger in arms, weaker in reach. I can use that.

Then the Dalidnon shaman raises his staff.

"By blood and vow, the Rite begins!"

He strikes the ground. The sand trembles, the sound echoing through the cliffs.

The drumbeats explode.

Sidlaw lunges first.

In a flash of motion, his right arm sweeps low, feinting.

I catch it, twist, step aside. Sand bursts beneath our feet.

He pivots, his fist grazing my ribs, hard enough to bruise. I answer with my fist to his shoulder, a strike to his chest, a driving kick that forces him back a step.

The crowd roars.

We move blow for blow, breath for breath. Every strike ripples across the sand.

He grabs my arm, tries to throw me.

I twist with him, break the hold, sweep his legs. Sidlaw crashes to one knee but surges up again, eyes blazing.

"Strong," he mutters. "Stronger than rumor."

"Alive, Prince," I say, breathless. "That's what the gods decided."

He grins through blood. "Then let's see if they favor you still."

He charges.

I brace, meeting him head-on. Sand sprays around us, the air filling with shouts and prayers. His fist slams into my jaw. I counter with an elbow to his ribs, feel the bone crack. He staggers, spits blood, and comes again.

Around us, the people chant. Two names, colliding like thunder.

Nogas! Sidlaw! Nogas! Sidlaw!

But all I hear is her voice in my head, like a gentle whisper through the breeze.

Please, Nogas. Please don't leave me again.

I can't look at her.

If I do, I will fall.

Sidlaw drives his shoulder into my stomach, slamming me back into the sand. The breath leaves my lungs. The sky reels. I roll aside as his fist hits where my head was a heartbeat before, sand erupting between us.

We both rise. Blood runs from his lip, from my nose. We breathe in time, two hearts pounding to the same terrible rhythm.

This is not hate.

This is inevitability.

Two men caught in the storm of gods and kings, fighting for the same woman.

But I don't fight to own her.

I fight to set her free.

I look up. The sun catches the sea.

It's blinding. Brilliant.

Burning.

Then I move.

Faster than thought.

Faster than breath.

And the fight truly begins.

CHAPTER 39

Walk to the Sun

Anini

EVERY BREATH I TAKE FEELS BORROWED.

They stand in the ring of sand, Sidlaw and Nogas, bare to the waist, their skin painted by the sea and the sun. Around them, the cliffs of Tinigbasan burn with banners. The lords watch from their seats of polished wood and stone. My father sits at the center, his face carved from worry.

I sit beside him, the golden veil of my robe pooling at my feet.

Nogas had bowed to me before the fight.

This is where your freedom begins, he said.

Those words have not left me since.

I see him now, scarred, silent, body coiled like a drawn bow. Every part of him seems honed to one purpose. He moves as if the gods themselves whisper in his pulse. Sidlaw, in contrast, is calm, his stance wide, shoulders loose, eyes clear as morning after a storm.

Two kinds of strength stand before the world.

They move like storm and tide. Each movement is precise, every strike beautiful in its violence.

It's not a brawl. It's a language of fists and breath and will.

I watch Nogas strike low to Sidlaw's ribs, but Sidlaw takes it, then retaliates with an elbow to the jaw that snaps Nogas' head to the side. I flinch. Blood arcs from his mouth.

But Nogas doesn't stop. He never stops. He circles, waits, studies. Sidlaw presses the advantage, driving him back with knee, fist, shoulder.

The sand darkens beneath their feet.

Sidlaw feints left, lands a right. Nogas stumbles, falls to one knee. My breath catches. The crowd gasps. He rises again, swaying, eyes fixed on Sidlaw.

Then, for a heartbeat, they move to me.

His look cuts through the roar, through the chaos.

It's not a plea. It's a promise.

Then he smiles, that reckless smile that once undid me while we fought together on the road.

And, finally, I understand.

Nogas moves. Sidlaw throws another punch. He ducks beneath it, then slips around Sidlaw's back in a blur of motion.

The same movement I saw once before, in another fight, another lifetime. His arm snakes around Sidlaw's neck. His other locks across the jaw.

The same hold. The same ending.

The Rite of Binding Blood at the river temple.

Sidlaw struggles. Once, twice, then again. His muscles

strain, veins rising under his skin. His eyes burn with defiance, refusing to yield. He pounds at Nogas' forearms, trying to wrench free.

Nogas tightens the grip. His face is stone, his body shaking with effort. The sound is terrible—the sound of strength straining.

Sidlaw's movements falter. His knees give way. His fingers slacken.

Then he goes still, his limp body sliding from Nogas' grasp.

The Dalidnon shaman rushes to Sidlaw, placing his hand to throat, to heart, but I can't hear the words. The crowd surges like a wave, shouting, weeping, praying.

My world has narrowed to one man standing in the center of the ring, dripping blood and breath and sunlight.

Nogas.

He doesn't lift his arms in triumph. He only straightens, chest heaving, gaze lost somewhere beyond the sky. When the shaman of Tinigbasan raises his staff, flanked by Oran and the shaman of Dalidnon, their voices boom over the sea.

"By the will of the gods, by the vow of the land and the sea! Nogas of Dumalog is the victor!"

The roar that follows is deafening.

But he doesn't move.

Nogas refuses the hands that reach for him. When they try to steady him, he shakes his head, the gesture weary but proud.

He turns, and I see him coming toward me.

My father's hand clamps around my wrist.

"Stay where you are!" he commands.

But I'm already moving.

I break free, running down the steps, through the wall of guards and servants. Someone shouts my name. I don't stop. My heart is a drum in my throat.

Nogas stumbles halfway to me.

I reach him just as he falls.

He collapses into my arms. His weight drives us both to our knees. His blood spills warm and heavy down my sleeves, soaking the gold until it turns crimson.

"Nogas…"

He lifts his face. The world blurs around him, all fading behind the roughness of his voice.

"Anini," he says, each word like breath broken, "as the rightful ruler of Hamtic, I release you from your duties as Princess of Tinigbasan."

My father shouts something. I can't hear it.

"This land," Nogas continues, voice shaking, "will no longer be known as such, but it will remember your name. *Anini*."

Tears slip down my cheeks. "Don't, Nogas. Please—"

"I give you the freedom," he says, "to choose your path. Your life. Your future."

His blood is everywhere. His eyes are fever-bright and beautiful. He turns then, still leaning against me, facing the stunned assembly of kings and their people.

"This is my first decree as your sovereign," he declares, voice hoarse but rising, carrying across the cliffs. "My second, that the Dumalog shall stand as their own rightful kingdom. Any attack upon them shall mean the ruin of those who dare. And third, the mountain tribes and forest clans are no longer vassals to any throne. Any attempt to subdue them will be taken as an act of war against all of Hamtic!"

Gasps ripple through the crowd. The shaman of Tinigbasan cries out, calling for scribes. Scrolls are unfurled. Ink spills. The sound of hurried quills scratches through the din.

Then the world around us erupts.

My father rising, face white as ash. Datu Radul yelling for his son. Dalidnon guards swarming the ring to lift Sidlaw's body. Mion pushing forward with Oran and a sobbing Lira.

"Nogas, please," I say. "Let them help you."

He shakes his head. "No." His breath rattles. "I wish to walk…walk with my princess. One last time."

"One last —" My voice breaks. "No, don't say that. Don't…"

"Take me to the cliff," he says softly, as though asking for mercy. "Where it all began. Dismiss me as your shield there. It will honor me greatly."

The guards part before us without command. Mion's jaw clenches, but he doesn't stop us. Oran lowers his head, silent. Lira's sobs follow us like a prayer.

We walk, our steps slow and uneven, through the crowd of stunned faces. Every step leaves a trail of red behind. The sun catches the blood on his skin and turns it to fire. His arm is heavy across my shoulders, his weight sinking with every breath.

The sea wind rises.

The drums have stopped.

Only the waves remain.

At the edge of the path to the cliff, where the world first began for us, he pauses.

Nogas looks at me, smiling faintly, the sun catching in his eyes the color of the darkest river stones.

Then he says, "Now you're free, Anini."

Together, we walk into the light, his blood gleaming behind us like a road back to the sea.

CHAPTER 40

Last of Honors

Nogas

THE WORLD FEELS SLOW, AS IF THE AIR ITSELF IS afraid to move.

Each breath I take feels stolen from her.

Anini helps me up the slope. The earth glows faintly beneath our steps, the light of the springs ahead flickering like molten gold beneath the rocks. The scent of salt and soil fills the air, the same scent as the day I first saw her.

We reach the cradle of the hot springs. Steam rises in silken ribbons, glimmering where the sun breaks through the clouds. The water murmurs softly. The petals floating upon it are bright and trembling, white and yellow.

It's the river-meets-the-sun blossoms.

I smile and say, "You grew them here, my love."

Anini kneels beside me, her hair catching the light as she nods.

"Yes, they grew where the spring broke through," she tells me softly. "Where the land remembered. Where the gods answered my heart's only wish."

Her voice is steady, but her hands shake as she helps me lower myself beside the water. I can feel the heat on my skin, the pulse of the earth beneath my palms.

"May we sit here?" I ask. "Just for a while. On the flowers."

She nods, unable to speak. Then she unclasps her golden cloak, now heavy with my blood, and wraps it around my shoulders, tucking the folds as though they could hold me together.

The warmth is not enough.

But her touch is.

I pull her close, my arms trembling, my breath shallow. "I've completed them, haven't I?" I murmur against her hair. "The three rites…The Binding Blood. The Living Land. The Shaping Sea."

Her fingers clutch at me. "Yes. Yes, you have."

"I remade the world," I tell her. "With hope. For you. Always for you."

She shakes her head, tears slipping onto my chest. "Don't speak as if it's over. Please."

But it is. The sun glints off the water like thousands of tiny mirrors, as if the sea itself wants to carry my last reflection. My body feels lighter now, floating in the shelter of her embrace.

"Anini," I breathe. "Live for both of us."

She presses her forehead to mine. "I will."

"Promise me," I say, the words scraping out of me, raw and breaking. "Promise you won't let them chain you. Not the title. Not the gods. Not grief."

Her tears fall faster. "I promise."

"Good." I reach up, fingers brushing her cheek. "Then you have given me peace. It's all I ever wanted."

The edges of the world begin to blur. The sound of the sea softens. The light becomes too bright to bear.

I try to smile for her. "I love you, Anini."

Her sob is small, almost strangled. "Nogas, don't. Please, Nogas."

"I think…" My voice catches. "I think it's time to dismiss me as your shield."

Her breath shakes, but she straightens, her palms framing my face. The words come out broken, but beautiful.

"You have given and taught me love," she says, voice trembling. "You have brought me honor. And hope. And freedom. Choice, above all."

She presses her lips to my forehead, her tears falling into the space between us. Then she kisses my lips. Her breath tastes sweet, like the tender fall of blossoms.

"The world will never forget your name because of it. I love you, Nogas. You are free. You will always be free."

The light around her blurs.

I feel her warmth one last time.

The sound of her voice fades into the rush of the spring. Into the scent of the sea, the sun, the river.

Everything I have ever fought for.

And then…peace.

The world breathes out.

The water stills.

Her heartbeat is the last sound I hear.

I let go.

EPILOGUE

The Home of the River

THE SEA IS PEACEFUL TONIGHT.

The air carries the same scent it always has. Salt, earth, and the faintest memory of smoke.

I walk the path up the cliff slowly, my staff tapping against the rock, the sound a steady rhythm, like the pulse of a remembered heart.

It has been many sun-cycles since the Rite of Binding Blood.

Sun-cycles since the world remade itself in light and stone and sea.

They call me shaman of the river temple now. Keeper of the springs, reader of the waters, voice of the land.

But tonight I am only a woman making her final journey home.

I have returned to Anini, the land that bears my name.

The kingdom once ruled by my father now belongs to Sidlaw's son, Datu Sarul, a just man, kind like his father, brave like the mother he lost too soon.

Sidlaw ruled well, but he was never the same after the Rite. Although he'd lived, neither he nor his father ruled the seas as they once did. But he made peace with the Dumalog and honored oaths our ancestors never had the courage to make. Once my father died, he united the kingdoms of Dalidnon and Anini. I mourned him when he passed, as one mourns a brother.

It feels strange walking these paths again. The guards and scholars of the river temple wait by the trees at the bottom of the cliff, burdened with my scrolls and inkstones, the exchange I make every season when I come to collect the writings of the coast and return the new ones I've transcribed in the temple.

I know this is my last visit.

I feel it in my bones.

"Stay here," I tell them. "I wish to greet the springs alone."

"Please let me come with you, great lady," says Captain Larsin.

"No, thank you," I tell him gently.

He nods and smiles. Larsin, the grandson of Lira and Mion, is the captain of the River Temple Guard. He carries his grandfather's calm and his grandmother's sharp mind.

The rest of the guards obey, but I feel their hesitation. Out of duty, perhaps, or maybe love. Most of them are orphans raised and taught under my wing, trained by the combat masters of Kalisidlan and Dumalog to serve a greater purpose.

Their footsteps and voices fade behind me.

Only the sea remains.

The light is soft and dying as I reach the summit. The

sky burns with the last colors of day, gold deepening to crimson, crimson to violet, violet to the first star. The spring still bubbles where it always has, clear and warm and eternal, surrounded by flowers of white and yellow.

River-meets-the-sun.

It was shortly after the Rite of Binding Blood when I found out these flowers grew on Nogas Island too. The pyre for Nogas was held there; he was mourned and celebrated by thousands upon thousands from tribes and clans all over the isles and mountains.

They call him the last true King of the Sea. I gave the Dumalog his shield and spear, but I kept his belt and daggers. I have carried his blades in all my travels. I still wear them, even until now.

I take off my sandals and dip my feet into the water. It sighs against my skin, the warmth spreading up my legs, through my chest, into the spaces grief once hollowed. I pluck one flower from the water's edge, tracing its petals with trembling fingers.

"I've come home, my love," I whisper to the bloom.

The wind moves through the cliffs, gentle, almost tender.

I close my eyes.

"Nogas," I murmur, "come get me. I've lived long enough. I have seen kingdoms rise and fall, watched peace blossom where blood once ran. I have travelled the world, taught the young, tended the river, written all that we were and all that we dreamed. I have lived for both of us. I kept my promise."

The flower drifts from my fingers, carried by the current.

"I want to be with you now," I say softly, my voice

breaking in the stillness. "In the realms beyond the sea and the sky."

The water stirs.

Ripples form, slowly, circling the spring in widening rings. The air hums, the light deepens, and from the heart of the spring, she rises.

Lady Kala's form glimmers between shadow and radiance, her long dark hair flowing like the ocean at dusk. She stands above the water, smiling the way the tide does before it takes what it loves.

"My dearest Anini," she says. "He has been waiting."

My throat tightens.

"Thank you," I say. "For everything. My story ends here, great lady. I want to be with my love now."

Kala steps closer, the water curling up her arms like silk. She reaches for my cheek, her touch cool and kind. "Then it is time to come home."

I nod. "The river is ready to meet the sun."

The world grows brighter. The sea below hums. The sky flares with gold. The springs glow as if catching fire. The petals around me rise into the air, spinning like tiny suns.

And then he's there.

Nogas.

Standing at the edge of the water, just as I remember him, smiling, sunlight in his eyes. The scars are gone. There is no more blood, no burden.

Only the man remains.

My shield. My blade.

My peace.

"Anini," he says, and it sounds like hearing my name for the first time.

I laugh, though tears stream down my face. "You took your time."

He smiles that same impossible smile. "I had to make sure the world remembered you first."

"And I made sure it remembered your name, my love," I say. "And everything you fought for."

Kala smiles and fades back into the water, leaving us bathed in gold.

I take a step closer, and Nogas holds out his hand. His fingers are warm and real. When they close around mine, everything that ever hurt finally goes still.

"Are you ready?" he asks softly.

I take his hand. "Yes."

And the river finally meets the sun.

ABOUT THE AUTHORS

Shirley Siaton Parabia is an award-winning author in English, Filipino, and Hiligaynon. She has several fiction and poetry books published since early 2023. *My Only Midnight* (October 2025) is her first Young Adult novel, while *River Meets the Sun* (October 2025) is her first YA collaboration.

Shirley is a black belt in Shotokan Karate and an international certified fitness coach. She works in education, wellness, and publishing. She lives with her family in the Sultanate of Oman, where she is writing her next book.

shirleyparabia.com

Peter Cordova Parabia is a proud son of Anini-y, Antique, Philippines, born and raised in the village of Igtumarom. *River Meets the Sun* (October 2025), a high fantasy retelling of his hometown's mythical origins, is his first book.

Peter has a career in teaching and Facilities Management. He is an accomplished athlete in bodybuilding and martial arts, with a black belt in Shotokan Karate. He is based in Muscat, Sultanate of Oman, with his wife and two daughters.

peterparabia.com

ON THE WEB

Shirley's official website:
shirleysiaton.com

Complete reading guide:
shirley.pub

Subscribe to Shirley's VIP list for free exclusive updates:
newsletter.shirleysiaton.com

www.ingramcontent.com/pod-product-compliance
Lightning Source LLC
Chambersburg PA
CBHW061219310726
48971CB00007B/1869